"Why are you ar

Guilt. Fear. Love. H̶̶̶̶̶̶̶̶̶̶̶̶̶̶̶̶̶̶̶̶ any of them and been speaking the truth. But then he'd have to explain something that defied explanation. The damn secret society...

"I'm worried about you," he said. "You're in danger."

If she was worried about him falling for her again, it was already too late—no matter that they had no future.

"You keep leaving," she reminded him, "you just take off, with no warning, with no explanation of where you're going or where you've been."

"I have patients. I have a responsibility to them." No matter *what* they were.

"What about us? You can't protect me if you're not here."

"I'll be here," he vowed.

Books by Lisa Childs

Silhouette Nocturne

Haunted #5
Persecuted #14
Damned #22
Immortal Bride #59
Mistress of the Underground #84

LISA CHILDS

has been writing since she could first form sentences. At eleven she won her first writing award and was interviewed by the local newspaper. That story's plot revolved around a kidnapping, probably something she wished on any of her six siblings. A Halloween birthday predestined a life of writing paranormal and intrigue.

Readers can write to Lisa at P.O. Box 139, Marne, MI 49435, or visit her at her Web site, www.lisachilds.com.

MISTRESS OF THE
UNDERGROUND
LISA CHILDS

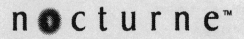

 **SILHOUETTE BOOKS**

ISBN-13: 978-0-373-61831-6

MISTRESS OF THE UNDERGROUND

Recycling programs
for this product may
not exist in your area.

Dear Reader,

I am so thrilled to be writing for Silhouette Nocturne. I'm especially happy to be back in the city I created in my Nocturne Bite, *Secret Vampire Society*, and revisited in "Nothing Says Christmas Like a Vampire," which appeared in *Holiday with a Vampire III*.

In *Mistress of the Underground*, Paige Culver discovers the Secret Vampire Society, but no mortal can learn about that secret group and continue to live. Unless that mortal is Dr. Benjamin Davison, Paige's ex-husband, who has reluctantly become the surgeon to the supernatural.

Ben can heal beasts, but his secret life prevented him from saving what mattered most to him—his marriage. When attempts are made on Paige's life, Ben tries to protect her but worries that he's only endangering her more. To save her, he might have to finally let her go.

I hope you enjoy your return to the Underground with Paige and Ben.

Happy reading!

Lisa Childs

To Tara Gavin, my amazing editor, who always understands how important my characters are to me. Thank you so much for giving me the opportunity to tell Paige and Ben's story!

Chapter 1

You don't belong here....

The skin tingled on the nape of Paige Culver's neck, and she shivered. To assure herself she was alone, she glanced around her small, windowless office. Light penetrated the green glass shade of the lamp on her desk but didn't dissipate the shadows clinging to the worn-brick walls.

You don't belong here....

That voice wasn't real; it had to be only in her head. Her own voice verbalizing the doubts that had tormented her since she'd bought Club Underground. She was a lawyer. What the hell did she know about running a lounge?

Actually, she wasn't a lawyer anymore—at least not one with a firm where she could practice. So she'd bought the club, which occupied the basement of a traditional brick office building in downtown Zantrax, the city which had replaced Detroit as the urban metropolis of Michigan. The building was the only thing traditional about Club Underground.

Music throbbed through the sound system, tempting Paige to leave the office and join the action. She pushed paperwork aside and stood up, swaying slightly on her stilettos as nerves assailed her again.

Opening night. Actually, reopening night, under new management, but yet she'd hidden herself back here, away from the club patrons. Would everyone else think, as she did, that she did not belong here?

"To hell with them," she murmured with the flash of pride and stubbornness that sometimes irritated the people she cared about. And to hell with what she thought, too. "There's no turning back now…."

With a slightly trembling hand, she smoothed down her flyaway strands of blond hair. Then she smoothed her hands over her hips, settling the red silk against her body.

Would *he* be out there? Waiting to congratulate her? Or to question her sanity? She didn't care which, as long as he was near—close enough to touch.

Anxious now, she hurried from the office, barely remembering to turn the lock before pulling the door closed behind her. In the hall, the music played louder, the bass lower and sexier. She glanced toward the door that separated the hall from the lounge. Then she glanced back the other way. To the door in the brick wall at the end of the hall. The door that led nowhere—according to the club manager. Then why was it locked?

You don't belong here....

The voice had to be inside her head; how else could she have heard it over the volume of the music? She shivered again, but from cold, not fear, and considered unlocking the office to retrieve her sweater. But it would ruin the effect of the dress with its thin straps and low neckline.

She didn't regret her decision, at least regarding the sweater, as she stepped into the lounge.

It would have been out of place, would have made *her* look more out of place than she already felt among the bodies gyrating on the dance floor. She didn't have the tiny waist or sharp curves of the women; her curves were rounder, fuller. And she was so much older, not just in years but in experience, than those laughing, flirting girls.

They were twenty-one, at least, or they wouldn't have been allowed inside the club. But no lines creased or dark shadows touched their clear skin. Self-conscious, Paige lifted a hand to her cheek. From her sleepless nights, she had dark circles and lines of stress. Not just because of her impetuous purchase...

But because of *him*...

She glanced around the bar in the lowest level of the turn-of-the-century building. Like her office, the outer walls were exposed brick, and the interior ones were dark paneled and as highly polished as the hardwood floors. The lights were dim, candles on the intimate tables and booths, strobes flashing sexily across the dance floor. She recognized no one among the crowd. Had none of her friends shown up to wish her well? Of course, she hadn't given them much notice about the club. She hadn't told anyone about what had been going on in her life. Not even he knew *everything*.

He knew *nothing*—actually, not a thing about this woman…but that she was gorgeous. The muscles tightened in Ben's gut as he studied her moving around the club, as bright and fluid as a flame. He tracked her through the crowd. In her red dress, with her golden hair, she stood out among the others with their dark clothes and their darker agendas. She didn't belong…for so many reasons.

"Hey—"

He ignored the voices calling out and the hands reaching for him and slipped through the crowd, following her. She glanced back, as if aware of his presence. From the first moment they'd met, they had always had an uncanny awareness of each other.

But she didn't stop walking. The sway of her hips, as she maneuvered through the crowd of club patrons, seduced him. He wanted to talk to her.

Who the hell was he kidding? He just wanted her.

Finally, he caught her—near the bar. She

leaned over it, shouting out an order to the bartender. And he leaned against her, his hands sliding over the soft curve of her hips. Silk brushed across his palms, and his skin tingled from the heat of her flesh. He wanted the silk gone—the crowd gone. He wanted only her and him—and skin on skin.

Despite the heat of the crowded club, and his touch, Paige shivered. Her heart kicked against her ribs with excitement...and anticipation. "I'll be out of your way in just a minute," she murmured over her shoulder.

"Out of my way?" his deep voice rasped in her ear.

His warm breath raised goose bumps along her nape, and she nodded. "So you can get your free drink."

"Free drink?"

"Opening night special," she explained. "First drink is on the house."

"What if I don't want a drink?"

She tilted her head so that her gaze met his. His eyes, big and dark and fringed with thick lashes, studied her intently. His hair was dark, too, but for the strands of gray sprinkled throughout; it was also cut short, but not so short that she couldn't run her fingers through its softness.

"Is there something else you—" she swiped the tip of her tongue across her bottom lip "—want?"

His fingers flexed against her hips, digging gently into her flesh. "I want the *special.*"

"I haven't told you the special," she reminded him with a teasing smile.

"I know what's special," he said, his gaze intent on her face.

Sadness tugged at her, pulling down the corners of her lips. If only she could believe him…but she knew better. If only she knew *him* better…

But they were strangers.

She whirled away from the bar and shoved past him. He caught her wrist, but she tugged free and slipped through the crowd. Voices murmured complaints as she bumped into hard bodies in her haste to escape him—and them— and that voice inside her head that pursued her all the way back to the office.

You don't belong here….

Paige's fingers trembled, and her keys jangled, as she pulled them from her small spangled clutch. She glanced to the end of the hall and that strange locked door.

Was the voice not inside her head? Was it coming from behind that door? The door that supposedly led nowhere? Now her legs trembled slightly as she passed the office and continued down the hall—toward that riveted steel door. When she neared it, still several feet away, cold air rushed around or through the steel and over her skin. She gasped and shuddered.

Then arms wrapped around her as a hard, warm body pressed against her back. And she screamed.

"No one can hear you," he said, his voice a deep rasp in her ear as his lips brushed the lobe. "Not back here, not over that music…"

Even though her heart raced, her lips curved into a smile. "Are you threatening me?"

"Warning you…"

He'd warned her before, but she hadn't heeded. Then. Now she was older and wiser. She knew this was the last man with whom she should get involved. Yet, instead of pulling away, she turned in his arms. He was taller than her, nearly a foot, with broad shoulders testing the seams of his black sweater. He wore all black:

black shoes, black pants and that black sweater with the sleeves pushed up to his elbows. He could have been a cat burglar or a stalker.

She should have been afraid, and part of her was, her stomach quivering as she acknowledged the danger of what she was about to do, the risk she was taking. But she didn't care. She lifted her hands to his chest, settling her palms against the sculpted muscles. Heat and the rapid beat of his heart emanated through the thin cashmere.

"You're not going to listen to any warning," he said with a sigh of resignation, even as his dark eyes burned with desire. "No matter what I say…"

"You talk?" she teased, but her skepticism was real.

His mouth, wide and sensual, lifted in a slight grin. "What's the point when you won't listen?"

She lifted her shoulders in a slight shrug, which drew his attention to the skin bared by her low bodice. His eyes darkened even more as his pupils dilated. Desire thickened her throat as she murmured, "There is no point to talking…."

She didn't want to talk or listen or think. She wanted the rush of passion pounding through her veins to drown out the voice and her doubts—not just about buying the club but about *him*.

His hands loosened their grip on her waist, but before he could step back, she reached up and clutched his shoulders. Then she lifted her face to his. For his kiss.

Instead of lowering his head to hers, he shook it. Then he manacled her wrists and pulled her hands away from him. He glanced over her head, at that steel door, and a shudder rippled through his hard, muscled body. "Not here."

"You…you feel it, too?" she asked.

"I feel *this* between us—" he released a ragged sigh "—even though I don't want to…."

"I don't want to, either," she insisted, even as her skin heated with desire for him. She tugged her wrists free of his hands and fumbled inside her bag once again for her keys. After jabbing the key in the lock, she turned the knob and opened the door to her office.

Just as at the bar, strong hands slid over her hips. Then he pushed her through the doorway and closed and locked the door behind them. Locking them inside the small, windowless room. Alone.

Her pulse quickened with excitement, but

her stinging pride tamped down that excitement. "I thought you didn't want to…that you didn't want…me…."

He leaned back against the door, his arms crossed over his muscular chest. "Yup, you never listen…." He sighed again. "I didn't say that I don't want you."

"But that you don't want to want me." She listened; too bad he hadn't ever really talked to her before.

"This is so complicated, Pai—"

"Shh," she said, interrupting him, reminding herself that she didn't want to talk or listen anymore. "You don't know my name, and I don't know yours. We're just strangers who met at a bar."

"Is that the game we're playing this time?"

It wasn't a game, not really. "We are strangers," she repeated.

"You don't want this, either," he pointed out, "or you wouldn't have run away from me at the bar. You nearly ran me over trying to get away from me." He shook his head and clicked his tongue against his teeth. "Hell of a way to treat your customers."

"Are you a customer?" she asked, fighting the smile that teased her lips.

He lifted a brow, dark with just a touch of gray. "Maybe not," he said, his voice a deep rumble. "I haven't had my free drink."

"Why not?" she asked, leaning against the edge of her desk because her knees trembled. She blamed the high heels; she wasn't used to wearing them anymore. "Can't you decide what you want?"

"That's never been *my* problem," he insisted as he straightened away from the door and advanced on her.

She didn't care what he was implying because he was wrong. She knew exactly what she wanted. Him, closer. Close enough to touch.

"I know what I want," he said, his hands closing over her bare shoulders, his fingers toying with the thin spaghetti straps of her dress. He wanted to talk. Just talk. That was what he'd told himself as he'd descended the stairs to Club Underground.

But now, touching her, her skin silky soft beneath his fingertips, he wanted only her. He pushed down the straps of her dress, exposing more of the luscious slopes of her breasts. "You are so beautiful…."

Her lips curved into a self-deprecating smile. "Back here—where it's just you and me. But not out there—among all those beautiful young girls."

"You're beautiful," he insisted.

"But I'm no young girl."

And neither were most of her patrons. But he couldn't point that out to her without having to explain things that defied explanation.

"You're a woman." *His* woman.

"For a guy who doesn't like to talk, you're talking too much now," she complained, but with another smile. Then she reached for his waist and slid her hands beneath his sweater, scraping her nails up his abdomen.

Ben shuddered again—this time for a good reason. Because only her touch could incite his desire to the point that he forgot everything else going on in his life and everything that had happened between them.

He lowered his head to hers. "Paige…"

"Shh…" she murmured as she kissed him.

The silkiness of her lips, the sweetness of her mouth, seduced him further, so that his control slipped. His hands shook as he gripped her waist and lifted her onto the desk. She lifted her legs, sliding her calves up the back of his thighs and over his butt to lock around his waist.

His cock hardened, throbbing behind the straining fly of his jeans. He pushed his hips forward, pressing against hers. She arched into him—as if there were no clothes between them…or secrets…or pain….

Only passion. It pumped through Ben's body, fast and heavy, and elicited a groan from deep in his throat. Paige answered him with a moan, and her hands clutched at his sweater, dragging it up his body.

He pulled his mouth from hers as she yanked the cashmere over his head and tossed it onto the floor. He fumbled with the clasp at the back of her dress, unhooking it before dragging down the zipper. As the red silk fell away from her body, his breath caught in his lungs, then escaped in a ragged gasp. "Damn it, woman…"

She wore no bra beneath the dress, so her breasts, so round and full, were bare to his hungry gaze. "You only get more gorgeous."

"And you get more charming," she said with a smile, as if she didn't believe his compliment.

But he'd never lied to her…except by

omission. There was so damn much he'd omitted over the years.

If she wouldn't believe what he told her, he'd have to prove it to her with his desire. He cupped her head in his hands, holding her face still for his kiss, for the possession of his mouth as he pressed her lips apart and slid his tongue across hers. She arched again, and her nipples rubbed against his bare chest.

Desire pounded in his head and his heart and he couldn't think rationally. He couldn't think at all…beyond the fact that he had to have her. He swept his arm across the desk behind her, knocking her papers and a cup to the floor. Ceramic cracked and broke, but he didn't care. He cared about nothing but her. Always her.

His hands shook as he fumbled with his zipper, pulling his pants down. And he took her. She was ready for him, wet and hot as he thrust inside her.

Her nails sank into his shoulders then scraped down his back, as she shifted and arched against him. He lowered his head and caught first one rose-hued nipple then the other in his mouth, laving it with his tongue.

Her fingers tangled in his hair as she pressed

his head to her breast. He reached between their bodies, sliding his fingers through her golden curls until he found the nub of her femininity. He pressed and stroked the pad of his thumb back and forth across it until she came, screaming against his lips as he kissed her deeply. His tongue slid in and out of her mouth, matching his rhythm as he moved in and out of her body. Her muscles clutched at him, holding him inside her.

And he came. He broke the rules of her little game—as he screamed her name. He couldn't pretend that they were strangers. He could only pretend that they could actually be together... even though he knew they had no future.

Chapter 2

Paige pulled her spaghetti straps back up her shoulders, making certain her dress wasn't on backward. The back dipped as low as the bodice. Warm lips brushed the bare skin between her shoulder blades. Shivering despite the heat racing through her, she leaned away and protested, "Only the first drink was on the house."

"Miss Kitty never kicked Marshal Dillon out of bed," Ben protested, then groaned as he flopped back down on the couch in her office.

The supple burgundy leather shifted beneath

him, nearly knocking Paige from where she perched on the edge, trying not to touch him again so that she would be strong enough to resist temptation. She smiled at his reference to the old western series about the female bar owner and the lawman. Late at night, after making love, they'd often watched reruns of the series.

"You're not Marshal Dillon," she told her ex-husband, who was actually a renowned cardiologist. But tonight, Dr. Benjamin Davison had been just a stranger in a bar. For these trysts, they usually pretended to be strangers. Unfortunately, they really weren't pretending despite having been married for ten years.

"And you're not Miss Kitty, Paige." He wedged his elbow behind his head, his dark eyes studying her. "This is crazy, you know…."

"Sleeping with you in my office? Yes, this is crazy," she agreed. But the craziness had everything to do with the fact that she'd never been able to resist him. She picked up his sweater from the floor and tossed it onto his chest, trying to conceal the wide expanse of hair-dusted muscles from her view.

To further steel her resolve, she stood up and

padded barefoot across the hardwood floor to her desk. She needed some distance between them—even though moving out and divorcing him hadn't given her nearly enough distance. Every time they'd run into each other in the four years since the divorce, they'd wound up in each other's arms. Her hands shook as she picked up the papers and files he'd swept to the floor.

"It is crazy," he agreed—a little too heartily for her pride. "I didn't come here for this…." He stood up and stretched, muscles rippling in his arms, chest and wash-board lean stomach.

Paige bit her bottom lip to hold in a lustful sigh; it wasn't fair. At forty-three, he was supposed to have a potbelly and love handles; he wasn't supposed to be as lean as he'd been in his twenties and thirties. She held in another sigh, a mingled one of relief and disappointment as he pulled on his pants and dragged his sweater over his head. His hair, the soft mixture of rich, dark chocolate and glittery silver, was mussed from the cashmere.

"So you came here for that free drink," she quipped, refusing to let him get to her again. *Still.* She had worked so hard to get him out of her heart; she couldn't let him back in. Because he had never let her in…

"I came here to talk to you," he said, "just talk."

She tensed, holding back the hope that threatened to rush over her. She could not allow herself to believe that he was really willing to share with her. During their marriage, he had shared very little of himself with her. "What do you want to talk about?"

"I want to know what the hell you're doing," he said, lifting a hand to gesture around the office. "I want to know why you quit the law practice and bought this club. What's going on with you?"

Despite having tamped down the hope, her heart constricted with regret. "*You* don't want to talk, Ben. You want *me* to talk."

"I want to understand you."

We don't always get what we want. She couldn't speak the words aloud, not without her voice cracking with pain. She'd wanted to understand him, too, so badly, but he'd never given her the chance.

"Why?" she asked. "Why now?"

"You're not acting like you."

And divorcing him, no matter how much she'd loved him, had been? And making love with him every time they had seen each other since?

"No, I'm not," she admitted, but he was the one who caused her to act out of character. Falling for him at all had been out of character; she'd known better than to risk her heart on anyone.

"What the hell are you doing?" he asked, dragging a hand over his hair, settling it back into place. "Why would you give up a career you love, that you lived for, for this?"

She'd lived for him, not her job. But she hadn't given up practicing law; the law practice had given up on her. Pride choked her, so that she couldn't admit she'd been fired. Finally she found her voice and injected a sassy edge, "Why not?"

"You don't belong here...."

She shivered in reaction to those chilling words. Was Ben's the voice she'd been hearing? "That's not fair," she murmured. He'd already messed with her heart; she couldn't have him messing with her head, too.

"You're cold," he observed, closing the distance between them with two strides. But he didn't touch her; he just stood close, so close that the silk of her dress brushed against his pants, the skirt swirling around his legs, binding them together. But even though there was so much binding them together, so much more kept them apart.

So many secrets. His. She had no idea what he kept from her; she just knew that he kept something. But more than secrets had caused their breakup—the loss and pain that they hadn't been able to share.

"Tell me why you would do this," he urged. "You have to know it's a mistake."

If so, it wasn't the first one she'd ever made. "I don't—"

"You know nothing about running any club," he said, "let alone one like this."

"Like what?" she asked as nerves fluttered in her stomach. "What's this club like?"

"You should have checked that out before you bought in," he criticized her.

And Ben had never criticized her—not even when she'd made the mistake that had cost them both so much. "That's not fair," she accused him again. "You have no idea what I did or didn't check out."

"I know you're not aware of everything about

Club Underground. I know because you wouldn't have bought it if you knew its secrets."

She gasped. "Secrets?"

The last thing she wanted in her life was more secrets—more answers just beyond her grasp. Like that voice that taunted her...

A fist hammered against the door, startling her nearly as much as his revelation. Apparently—from the way he'd closed his eyes and clenched his jaw—a revelation he regretted making.

"Paige!" a deep voice called through the door, "I have to talk to you."

She blew out a breath that stirred a lock of hair near her cheek. "Great. Usually nobody wants to talk...."

Ben's fingers skimmed along her jaw, tilting her face back to his, as he insisted, "Paige, we're not done."

Didn't she know it? They wouldn't be done until the day she summoned the willpower and strength to resist the sensual hold he had on her.

"I need to open the door," she said, her voice soft and a bit breathless as she struggled against the pressure in her chest, building with every word he spoke, every glance of his dark, mesmerizing eyes. "Ben..."

"You've made a mistake, Paige, just like you did when you…" He didn't finish, but he didn't need to. She knew what she had done. They both did. She'd accepted that she would never be able to forgive herself; now she realized that neither would he. Hell, she had always known that too much kept them apart. But now more than his secrets—that pain and loss stretched between them.

The fist hammered again, rattling the wood in the jamb.

"I need to get that," she said, stepping around her ex-husband to open the door before the club manager pounded it down.

But Ben called her back, "Paige…"

She ignored him to focus on Sebastian, the tall dark-haired man standing the doorway. Like Ben he wore black, but in a tailored suit. A silk tie, nearly as deep a red as blood, provided the only splash of color against a black shirt. "Hey, what's the emergency?" She hoped like hell there wasn't one, because she would have no idea how to manage it.

Sebastian Culver's dark blue eyes narrowed as his gaze moved from her to Ben, then back. "Am I interrupting anything?"

"Wouldn't be the first time," Ben remarked. He usually teased her younger half brother, but now his voice held a noticeable trace of bitterness.

She shook her head. "No, Ben and I were finished." A long time ago, and they needed to remember that. "Do you need me in the club?"

"Your friends are here," Sebastian said. "I put them at the quiet table in the back and set them up with drinks."

Her friends. Would they think, like Ben did, that she'd made a terrible mistake, that she didn't belong in Club Underground? She sucked in a breath, bracing herself to find out. She didn't glance back at Ben as she turned and walked away. But she did glance again at the door at the end of the hall.

In ten years of marriage, she had never learned Ben's secrets. She wouldn't live that way again. As soon as her friends were gone, she intended to find the key to that door and find out exactly what was hidden behind it.

Watching her walk away—again—had anger gripping Ben. He was used to the frustration and resentment he always struggled with when he was around Paige. But this time there was more, and his anger boiled over to Sebastian. He clenched his hand into a fist, tempted to slam it into the other man's handsome face. But he dragged in a deep breath and forced his fingers to relax. He hadn't controlled his urge for violence out of any affection for his ex-brother-in-law but because, as a surgeon, he couldn't risk injury to the instruments of his livelihood.

Even though he resented his career as much as he sometimes resented Paige, he couldn't do what she had. He couldn't give it up—no matter how much it had cost him. He didn't understand her leaving the law firm *now* when she'd had better reasons for leaving before. The resentment flared up again, twisting his gut. Despite all the years he'd known her and how much they were alike in some ways—like their lacking childhoods—he had never really understood Paige.

He grabbed the taller guy by the lapels of his tailored suit. "What the hell were you thinking— letting her get involved with Club Underground?"

Sebastian wrested free of his grasp and stepped back. "C'mon, Ben," he began with his patented charming grin.

He was too angry to listen, let alone be charmed. "We agreed to keep her away from here."

"Yeah, right, like either of us has ever been able to keep Paige from doing anything she wants."

Like divorcing him. She'd been the only one who wanted that, but he hadn't tried hard enough to change her mind. Hell, he really hadn't tried at all. He'd never been able to give her what she'd needed and deserved—all of himself.

"But why would she want to do this?" he asked, gesturing around the basement office. "You must have said something to her…something about the club closing."

Sebastian sighed and pushed a hand through his overly long black hair. "I did, but I never intended for her to get involved. I tried to get financing on my own, so that I could buy the club. But I didn't qualify and the place would have had to close down."

Ben flinched, blaming himself. He'd tried to save the previous owner, but he'd been in surgery at the hospital and hadn't gotten to the club in time. Sebastian hadn't asked him for the money, probably because he'd already cost Ben too much.

"So Paige came to the rescue." As she had often rescued her brother and anyone who'd been fortunate enough to have her representing them in court.

"You two have that in common," the other man told him. "You're both rescuers."

Ben shook his head, refusing to let Sebastian diffuse his anger with compliments. Especially unfounded ones. "We both know that's not true—or the club wouldn't have been at risk of closing."

"You did everything you could. More than anyone else could have done," Sebastian assured him, then patted his own chest. "I'm living proof of your skills."

"Okay, I understand her giving you the money." Because how could anyone refuse this man anything? "But why'd she have to quit her job and get involved in the day-to-day operation?"

Sebastian shrugged. "I guess you're not the only one keeping secrets now."

"I've never been the only one keeping secrets," Ben reminded his ex-brother-in-law. "You've got to get her out of here. It's not safe for her to be here."

The other man nodded. "I know that. What I don't know is how to get her to leave."

"You have to think of something," Ben insisted. "She's going to get hurt. Just being here puts her in danger."

"You think I don't know that?" Sebastian's usually smooth voice vibrated with frustration and fear. "You're the only mortal who can know the truth and live."

Ben snorted with derision. "That's hardly an honor." Knowing the secret had ruined his life and his marriage.

"It's a necessity," Sebastian admitted. "You're a necessity."

"So can't I barter for her protection…?"

Sebastian shook his head. "You don't think I tried?"

"But I have more leverage than you do," Ben pointed out, with no pride. "I'm the only one who can keep the undead really undead."

Sebastian pressed his hand against his chest, as if to assure himself that his heart still beat. "Don't I know…"

"Don't they know that?" Ben asked, frustration clenching the muscles in his stomach. "Don't they remember what I've done for them—for most of them?"

"They respect the hell out of you, Ben. Nothing's going to happen to you. But…"

"So doesn't that respect give me leverage to protect Paige?"

Sebastian shook his head. "Not now. You two aren't together anymore."

He could argue about that since they had just been very together. But they now lived separately. Hell, even when they'd been married, they'd lived separate lives.

"And that's because of this damn secret—this damn secret life I've been living," Ben said, the frustration threatening to consume him now.

"There's more to your breakup than that," Sebastian said, his voice soft with commiseration.

Ben closed his eyes on a wave of regret and pain. "I can save you—all of you—but I couldn't save my own. I couldn't save what was mine."

A strong hand closed over his shoulder and squeezed. "You have to stop blaming yourself."

"I—I can't…"

"That's something else you and Paige have in common then," Sebastian said. "You can't stop blaming yourselves—for things over which you had no control. And you have no control over this, Ben. No matter what you mean to the Underground community, the secret society, you can't protect Paige."

"Then *you* better." He jabbed his fingertip against Sebastian's heart—the heart from which Ben had removed a wooden stake a decade ago.

He had saved Sebastian's life but ended his own—at least the life he'd once known. The life to which he could never return.

As much as Paige needed to stay away from Club Underground, Ben needed to stay away from her. She only reminded him of all that he'd lost—and all that he could never have again.

Chapter 3

He was gone. Paige knew the moment Ben left Club Underground. Her pulse slowed and her skin stopped tingling. But even though he was gone, she could still feel his touch—could still taste him.

With a slightly trembling hand, she lifted the flute of champagne to her lips. She needed to wash away his flavor. If only she could wash away her feelings for him as easily.

"Wait!" Campbell O'Neil yelled over the music, which was too loud even at the *quiet* corner table. Then the redhead grasped Paige's arm, holding the glass just shy of her mouth. "We have to make a toast first."

"We have to wait for Kate before we do that," Dr. Renae Grabill leaned across the table to add.

Paige glanced around, hoping to catch a glimpse of the tall brunette in the crowd. She really needed a drink. And she really needed her friends—all her friends—but most especially Lieutenant Kate Wever. Perhaps the Zantrax major case detective could help her discover the secrets of Club Underground. "Is she working late?"

"She was here," Elizabeth Turrell said from where she sat at Paige's side. "Then she thought she recognized someone in the crowd."

"She knows someone here?" Renae asked doubtfully as she young trauma surgeon studied the bodies gyrating on the dance floor.

Campbell snorted. "A lot of these people look familiar to me, too."

Nerves fluttered in Paige's stomach. "It's probably not a good thing that a prosecutor and a detective think my customers look familiar."

"Your customers," Elizabeth mused. "*You* shouldn't be here. You should be back at the firm."

Paige met her friend's gaze; guilt darkened the other woman's brown eyes. "Lizzy…"

"It's my fault that you're not," Elizabeth said.

Paige squeezed the other woman's hand. "You can't blame yourself."

"No, blame that dick you married," Kate remarked as she joined the group of friends.

Lizzy's ex—and Paige's former employer—had fired Paige to spite Lizzy for finally finding the nerve to divorce him. He probably hadn't wanted to fire Elizabeth, who was a divorce lawyer at the firm, because he might have had to pay more child support. So Roger had fired his ex's friend instead. If Paige could have proved it, she would have sued him, but despite her suspicions and Lizzy's certainty, she'd had no proof. And no job.

"So was it him?" Campbell asked.

"Who?" Kate asked.

"Whoever you thought you recognized," the assistant D.A. reminded her.

Kate shrugged as if unconcerned, but her face was tense with distress, her skin drained of all color. "I don't know…." She drew in a shaky breath, then fixed her gaze on Paige's face. Her pale blue eyes narrowed. "I'm obviously not the only one who doesn't know what the hell she's doing. What were you thinking, Paige, to buy *this* place?"

Goose bumps rose on Paige's skin. So she hadn't imagined that there was something strange about Club Underground. "What is it about this place? What do you know?"

Kate shrugged again. "Nothing I can prove."

Elizabeth uttered a nervous laugh even as she shivered. "C'mon, Paige, don't let Detective Wever's cynical view of the world affect yours."

Paige sighed. "I actually have my own cynical view." And maybe that had colored her judgment regarding the club. If she didn't dare care about it too much, she wouldn't lose it, as she had lost everything else that mattered to her. First her father, then her mother, and more recently her husband, her career and her...

"Well, let's toast for a brighter view," Elizabeth suggested as she lifted the glass of champagne.

Kate lifted her glass, too, but she offered a warning instead of a toast. "We're not done yet. We can celebrate your new gig tonight, but we'll talk about it tomorrow."

Paige smiled. "I'm counting on that." She

needed to talk to Kate and find out what exactly the detective couldn't prove, but the club was too crowded and too loud for them to have the conversation they needed to have. Kate nodded, as if she'd read Paige's mind and had agreed to meet another time.

They were the kind of friends—all of them—who knew, instinctively, when she needed them and when she needed to be alone to regroup and recover. But even when they left her alone, they never completely left her—like so many other people in her life had.

"I'm so sorry that you got caught up in my personal mess," Elizabeth said.

"Stop apologizing." Paige slung an arm around Lizzy's shoulders and squeezed. "I didn't buy the club because I lost my job. I would have bought it had I still been working. Sebastian was looking for financing so he could buy it himself." He'd been managing the club for years, ever since he'd shown up at her door a decade ago. Until then, she hadn't even known she'd had a sibling, but she hadn't been surprised given her father's playboy reputation.

"Sebastian's always looking for something," Campbell remarked with a chuckle as, with her champagne flute, she gestured toward the dance floor.

Paige's younger brother, a mike clutched in his fist, moved among the dancers as he sang a haunting ballad of love lost. A chill chased up and down her spine as she connected with the song; she had lived it. While they hadn't grown up together, having had different mothers, Sebastian had been there for her when she'd needed him most. If not for his support, she might not have survived losing her love.

"You could have told him no," Renae said with a snort of disgust.

Campbell laughed again. "I doubt any woman has ever summoned the willpower to tell Sebastian Culver no." Apparently her brother hadn't fallen far from the paternal tree.

She had had the willpower but nothing else— so she'd thought she had nothing to lose. Nothing but money. Now she worried that something else was at stake here in Club Underground, like perhaps her life.

Once the door closed behind the last patron, the club fell eerily silent. The click of Paige's heels against the hardwood echoed as she walked down the hall toward her office. If she hadn't left her purse in her desk, she wouldn't have gone back because of the memories of what had happened earlier that evening.

She'd made another mistake—just the latest of many in her forty years. At least this time the only one who'd probably get hurt was herself.

She needed more. So did Ben. But the thought of no longer playing the sex games they'd been playing since shortly after their divorce filled Paige with dread. Her stomach churned at the prospect of dating real strangers, at having to weed through losers and potential serial killers to find a man she could trust as she trusted Ben. And the idea of never touching Ben, of never being with him again...

But even when they'd been living together, they'd never been *completely* together. From the day they'd met, Ben had always held a part of himself back from her. She'd excused it because he'd spent his childhood in foster homes, and because of his profession. He'd learned not to get attached, not to get involved. Her first mistake with him had been thinking it would be different with them, that she could love him enough to break down the wall he'd built around himself. Maybe she would have…had she been able to give him what he'd really wanted….

She pushed open the door Ben had left unlocked and dragged in a deep breath. The room smelled of him—that mixture of musk and leather and sweet cigars. But there was another scent she recognized. It could have been from him; he had often come home smelling of it after a particularly hellish night in the O.R.: death.

She glanced at her desk and noticed someone had brought in a flower arrangement. This was no congratulatory bouquet from her friends. The roses were black. A dozen of them, dried and dead, so brittle that petals dropped onto her files and closed laptop. The stems protruded from foam that someone had carved into a shape of a heart. But more than stems penetrated the foam: a wooden stake pierced the heart.

Hand shaking, she reached for the card that was stuck to the stake. Red ink, smeared like blood, spelled out the words: "You're going to get what you deserve."

She replaced the card and stepped out of her office. Once again a strange chill swept down the hall…from that maddeningly locked door. While that door was locked, her office hadn't been. Anyone could have left the hideous bouquet. "Sebastian!"

She wasn't afraid. She was tired.

"Paige! Are you all right?" Sebastian called out, his voice rough with emotion as he ran down the hall toward her.

"I'm fine," she assured him, unsettled that he'd been so easily rattled. Hopefully she hadn't sounded that upset; she refused to let some misguided joke or a case of nerves unsettle her. "I just found something in the office...."

"What? Another rat?"

They had found one the night she'd taken possession. She'd seen a rat in her office as a bad omen. And that had been even before she'd started hearing the voice telling her she didn't belong.

"There's no rat, just those," she said, pointing toward the black roses as she had the rat droppings, with disgust. "I hope you didn't waste your money on those hideous things."

"I didn't send them."

"What?" she asked, unsure if she should believe him. Along with his considerable charm, Sebastian had quite the sense of humor. "Yeah, right."

Hurt flashed in his bright blue eyes. "Paige, I wouldn't purposely do anything that might upset you, especially tonight."

She believed him but wished he was lying. "But if you didn't send them…"

Who had? The question raised all kinds of sinister possibilities in her mind.

Chapter 4

Ben's heart pounded against his ribs as he crashed through the unlocked door of Club Underground. He'd done this so many times, so many other nights, that he should have been used to the summons. But tonight was different—tonight he knew the emergency concerned Paige.

His hand shook so badly he had to tighten his grip on the handles of his medical bag. Sebastian had assured him that she wasn't hurt; Ben didn't need the bag. But he'd gotten used to carrying it with him as he never knew when he'd need it. Or when a member of that damn secret vampire society needed him.

As Ben walked into the dark bar, he called out for Sebastian.

"Down here," his ex-brother-in-law replied, his deep voice drifting from the hall.

Ben headed toward that door Paige had found so fascinating, but before he reached it, strong fingers grasped his arm.

"In the office," Sebastian said, tugging him inside the room he had not wanted to see again.

Hell, he never wanted to see any of Club Underground, but yet he came every time they called. Because he had no choice. And now Paige owned the place, which actually gave him another reason to stay away. He'd never brought her anything but pain. "Is she all right?"

"Yes. For now."

"What happened?"

"Those happened," Sebastian replied, pointing toward a bunch of black roses.

Ben noticed the stake embedded in the make-shift heart, and he understood the concern wasn't about the flowers. "What the hell. Someone's threatening Paige?"

Sebastian sighed. "After the bar closed down for the night, she found the arrangement in her office."

"An office she shouldn't even have here." Ben ran a trembling hand over his hair. "But why use the stake to threaten Paige? It makes no sense. She's not one of the society."

"Maybe that's the threat."

"That they'll make her into one of you? Then what? Kill her? It makes no sense," Ben said, frustration and fear gnawing at him.

"Sometimes it doesn't make sense," Sebastian reminded him. "Sometimes somebody needs no motive other than madness."

Ben shuddered, remembering the destruction he'd seen and tried to treat that had resulted from such madness.

He glanced at the flowers and the stake again. "There's a note?" He reached for it, but Sebastian pulled his hand back.

"It says she's going to get what she deserves."

"I want to see it," Ben said. "Maybe I'll recognize the handwriting."

"Don't touch it," Sebastian advised. "She wants to report this *special delivery* to Kate, the Zantrax major case detective."

Ben groaned. "If Paige reports this to her, it'll put them both in danger."

"I talked her out of calling Kate tonight, but I think that was just because she was too tired to argue with me. And she probably didn't want to wake up Kate." Sebastian pushed a hand through his hair. "She cares more about her friends than she does herself."

"She's never done very well taking care of herself," Ben remarked. "But neither of us did very well taking care of her, either."

Sebastian's face flushed with color and he protested, "Hey, that's not fair—"

"We almost lost her once," Ben reminded him. "Where is she now?"

"Home."

"Alone?" Pressure tightened the muscles in his chest as his fear for her safety conflicted with his fear that she might not be alone. Although they'd been divorced four years, he wanted her with no one but him. Which made him selfish as hell, since he couldn't give her what she deserved—happiness, security…

"She thinks she's alone," Sebastian said.

"But you have someone watching her?" Ben asked, the fear rushing back.

The other man nodded.

"Someone you can trust?"

Sebastian flinched. "You're the only one I really trust—"

"Damn it, you promised you'd watch over her—that you'd make sure she didn't get hurt." And Ben shouldn't have trusted anyone with that responsibility but himself. But, as Paige had often reminded him—when he'd tried to give her alimony—since he'd signed the divorce papers, she was no longer his responsibility.

"She'll be safe," Sebastian insisted. "The person watching her is too afraid to hurt her or to let her get hurt."

"Afraid of you?" Ben asked, arching a brow with skepticism. Sebastian had the reputation of being more of a lover than a fighter.

"Afraid of *you,*" the other man clarified.

"Then I should be the one protecting her," Ben said. The divorce hadn't stopped him from caring about her no matter how much Paige wanted to keep things light and impersonal between them. All sex and no emotion. He couldn't blame her after the way he'd hurt her.

Now he had to make certain no one else hurt her. He turned toward the door just as a guttural moan echoed down the hall. From all the years he'd been a surgeon, Ben readily recognized the cry of pain. While the cry was familiar, the voice was not. Ben grabbed his bag and hurried out to find his patient collapsed on the floor. Blood spurted between the fingers of the hand that the guy clutched against his throat.

"Son of a bitch," Sebastian murmured from behind Ben. "Is he mortal…?"

"I think we're about to find out." Someone could have tried "turning" the guy into a vampire, but that process proved such a risk. Ben had treated many mortals as they turned; he'd lost more of them than he'd been able to save.

He focused on this patient, refusing to lose another one—even while he worried that he might lose Paige. Again.

The sun had yet to rise when Paige returned to Club Underground. An outside light illuminated the cement steps leading down to the bar. Trying to sleep had been pointless—with all the thoughts racing through her mind and chasing her back here to reinspect that sinister flower arrangement. She hurried down the stairs, the skin pricking between her shoulder blades as if someone's gaze bored a hole in her back. Ever since she'd left her condo, she'd had that sensation, the one of being watched.

Her hand shook as she shoved the keys in the lock and opened the door. As she crossed the dance floor to the hall, her foot slipped and she fell, one leg forward, her other one folded beneath her. She sucked in a breath of pain over her forced splits. "What the hell…?"

She'd trusted Sebastian to supervise the cleaning crew, but one of the crew must have missed a spilled drink. She ran her hand across the polished floorboards, smearing something sticky across the wood and her skin. To identify the substance in the dim security lighting, she lifted her hand to her face. "Blood?"

And it wasn't just on the floor. A streak had spattered across the wall next to the door to the hall leading to her office. Fear clutched at her heart—not for herself but for her brother. Was Sebastian all right? She opened her mouth to scream his name, but then a noise—a bump and a clatter—echoed down the hall. From her office or the locked door?

She reached for her purse, and the cell phone inside it. But when she'd fallen the contents had spilled out and scattered across the floor. Tears of frustration stung her eyes; she needed to call for help. She scrambled to her feet and ran for the bar, moving behind it to the phone sitting next to the register.

Another bump and a mumbled curse echoed down the hall. Her hand passed over the phone, and she closed her fingers around the neck of a bottle instead. No matter who she called, they wouldn't arrive in time to protect her. She had to protect herself.

Adrenaline pulsing in every nerve ending, she headed around the bar to the hall—the liquor bottle clutched tight in her hand. Her flower sender was about to get his first round free— against the side of his head.

Paige stepped into the hall, brandishing the bottle as a weapon. But before she could swing at the shadow that stepped out of her office, strong fingers closed around her wrist.

"Damn it, Paige," the man remarked, "you almost got me with that. What the hell—"

"Ben!" She smacked his shoulder with her free hand. "What the *hell* are you doing here— besides scaring me half to death?"

"Hey, you're the one who nearly knocked me

out," Ben said. "I'm here because Sebastian asked me to come down."

"Is he all right?" she asked, glancing around her ex to search for her brother. However, the office was empty except for that gruesome flower arrangement.

"He's fine," Ben said. "He's already taken off."

"What about the blood out there on the dance floor? Is that his?"

Ben shook his head. "No. It wasn't his."

"What happened out there? Who got hurt?"

His broad shoulders lifted in a weary shrug. "I don't know. One of the cleaning crew must have cut himself. Sebastian didn't say anything about it."

"You didn't notice the blood?"

He shook his head again. "After all the years I've spent in an O.R., I guess I'm desensitized to it."

If only she could get desensitized to him…. Because where his fingers still gripped her wrist, her skin tingled and heat streaked throughout her body. She lifted her gaze to his face, and while his eyes darkened with desire, lines of fatigue radiated from them. And a dark shadow clung to his jaw.

"Why did you come back down here?" she asked. "You look like you need your sleep." But in all the time she'd known him, he'd never gotten enough rest. The man did not know how to *take it easy.*

His mouth shifted into a sideways grin, as if he was too tired to curve his lips into a complete smile. "Is that a nice way of saying I look like hell?"

She laughed. "Don't pretend I've wounded your pride. I'm sure there are plenty of females down at the hospital—staff and patients—who stroke your ego quite enough."

"Now you're calling me conceited."

"Conceited?" She paused as if considering and then shook her head. "Arrogant, yes." But not without damn good reason. The man had all kinds of talents. Thinking about the one he'd shown her in her office just hours before had heat flushing her skin.

He chuckled, as if he'd read her mind. Why hadn't he been able to do that when they'd been married?

Embarrassed and frustrated at her weakness,

she glanced away from him. Her gaze landed on the door at the end of the hall.

"You've done it again," she said.

"What?"

"Avoided answering my question." Maybe the divorce had been more his fault than hers. "Why did you come back down here, Ben?"

Anger replaced the flare of desire in his eyes. "Sebastian wanted me to see that opening-night gift you got."

Damn him. And damn Ben for coming. "And here I thought you'd developed such a drinking problem that you can't get enough."

"I can't seem to get enough of something, but it isn't alcohol," he admitted, his fingers stroking over her skin before he released her wrist. But he took the bottle, turning his attention to the label. "The hard stuff, huh?"

"If you're going to bean someone over the head, you better use the hard stuff." She stepped away from him, just resisting the urge to rub her wrist where his touch still burned her skin.

"You didn't think I was a desperate drunk," he scoffed at her claim, "you thought I was whoever left those flowers in your office."

"And the stake," she reminded him as she

walked over to her desk where the hideous arrangement remained, despite Sebastian's offer to get rid of it. Heck, he'd done more than offer; he'd insisted. She was surprised he'd listened to her when she'd explained that she wanted to hang on to it. "You know…all those years as a lawyer and the first time I'm called a vampire is after I'm no longer practicing law."

"You'll always be a lawyer, Paige," Ben insisted. "It's being a bar owner that you should probably rethink."

"Why are you so against my owning this place?" she asked, remembering that earlier he had seemed to have a problem with it.

His lips curved into that half grin again. "And see, more questions. You're a lawyer through and through, Paige. I don't understand why you would give that up now…."

"When I hadn't before when you wanted me to?" Regret and resentment overwhelmed her. She couldn't deal with him…or the flowers… not without losing it.

Chapter 5

Paige pushed past him and ran out in the hall. This time Ben didn't just watch as she walked away; he hurried after her. "I never wanted you to quit, Paige. I only wanted you to take it easy...to take care of yourself."

She'd had to take care of herself because he'd been too busy taking care of everyone—and *everything*—else. As he followed her into the bar area, he glanced at the blood on the dance floor and the wall.

That patient was a member of the secret

society. His girlfriend, also a society member, had gotten a little too passionate and nicked his carotid. While he wouldn't have died, necessarily, the blood loss had weakened him to the point of helplessness. Stitching the wound and administering a transfusion had brought back his strength—so much so that Sebastian had already taken him home and left Ben to clean up the mess.

Along with the blood, he'd been supposed to dispose of the flowers before Paige saw them again and followed through on her inclination to call the police. Hell, maybe she should; Ben hadn't protected her before. He didn't trust himself to protect her this time, either.

"I take care of myself," Paige insisted. "What happened…it was…"

Something they'd never talked about before. Even now, he couldn't find the words to express his regret and loss and pain. Instead he glanced down at the bottle he still held—the one with which she'd nearly clocked him. As softly and gently as he liked to caress Paige's naked skin, he ran his fingers over the label on the Dewar's bottle. *Hello, old friend…*

Scotch had brought him comfort many a night after Paige had left him. Too many nights.

If he'd had a little less control, he might have become dependent on alcohol. But he'd had too many people—both living and undead—depending on him. So he had fought off the temptation then, and he would do so now because Paige needed him. He had to stick close to her, to protect her without her realizing what he was doing.

God, sticking close to Paige...

His body hardened at the thought of being close to her again—as close as they'd been earlier in her office, him buried inside her. So that he didn't reach for her, he stepped behind the bar to place the bottle next to all the others. He'd been in Club Underground so many times—too many times—but he had never really noticed how elegant the club was. Appreciatively he ran his hand over the sparkling granite surface of the polished mahogany bar.

"If you're thinking about a career change, too, I could use another bartender," Paige offered.

"I could no more stop being a doctor than you could stop being a lawyer." Yet there had been times, since he'd learned of the secret society, that he'd wanted to quit. But they'd made it clear to him that the only way out for him was death.

She lifted and spread out her arms to encompass the darkened lounge. "Look around. No law books, not a contract in sight. I'm not a lawyer anymore."

"Why not?"

"You know," she scoffed. "You're too thick with my brother for him to have kept his mouth shut."

"He said it was your secret."

She arched a dark blond brow. "And you couldn't have gotten it out of him?"

He probably could have, but he wanted her to tell him. He wanted her to share her life with him. Shame washed over him at his selfishness. How could he expect her to share her life when he couldn't share his?

"I can't believe Sebastian dragged you down here over those flowers," she said, neatly avoiding his question as he had so many of hers over the years. "He was the one who told me they were nothing—that they'd probably been delivered to the wrong place."

It might have been what he'd said, but it wasn't what Sebastian believed. He hadn't wanted her to call the police because an investigation might uncover the secret society and put everyone at risk. Ben would have preferred that to having Paige at risk. He uttered a sigh of frustration. "He's probably right."

She nodded. "There is no other logical explanation."

Even if she learned the secret, she would never understand it. Paige had never been able to accept that some things defied logic.

"I'm sorry that you came down here for nothing," she said.

"How could I not?" he asked. "If you need me, I'll always be here for you."

Liar. She refrained from shouting at him, from letting all her resentment and pain spill out. He hadn't been there for her...when she'd needed him most. When she'd left the office earlier, she should have kept running; she shouldn't have let him stop her. "We both know better than that, Ben," she gently reminded him.

He flinched as if she had screamed at him. "You're right. You were right to leave me, too."

"Oh, Ben…" God, they weren't good for each other. They had nothing between them anymore but guilt and pain…and a crazy, irresistible attraction.

"I'm not Ben," he said, with a luminescent gleam in his big, brown eyes.

"Oh, you're not?"

He shook his head. "Who was I last night?"

"Stranger in a bar," she said, as if reading a role from a playbill.

"So today," he said as he ran his fingertips across the granite again, "I'm the lonely bartender."

Somehow she suspected "lonely" wasn't part of the role he wanted to assume, but already part of who he was.

"So who am I?" she asked him.

"Last night you were the sexy bar owner."

"Still am," she quipped, no matter that no one—including him—thought she belonged at the club.

His mouth lifted into a little grin. "No, today you're a patron who left her purse here and came back after hours to pick it up."

"I have a feeling that my purse is not the only thing I'm supposed to pick up," she said, her pulse quickening with excitement.

"I have your bag back here," he said, lifting the hinged counter so she could join him, "behind the bar."

She smiled now. "Did you get this scenario from a country song? I didn't think you listened to country."

"I listen to everything."

Even her? She shook her head. No, she would have had to talk for him to listen; he wasn't the only one who hadn't shared all his feelings during their marriage. She hung on to her smile, with an effort. "I thought you were just into that boring elevator music."

"Come here," he urged her, "and I'll show you how boring I am."

Weren't they fighting because he thought it was crazy that she'd bought the bar? She'd rather not remind him of their argument. Better to distract him or herself from her fear that he was right.

"You know you should be wearing the uniform," she said as she stepped behind the bar and walked toward him. She'd love to see him in the black pants and a pleated tuxedo shirt.

"I already changed out of uniform," he said, gesturing toward the black pants and sweater he wore. The ones that had lain on her office floor just hours before.

"Maybe you shouldn't be wearing anything at all," she suggested, reaching for the hem of his sweater. She dragged it up and over his head, tossing it onto the bar.

His chest was bare, except for the light mat of black hair covering the sculpted muscles. Despite his hectic schedule, he somehow found time to work out.

Paige put her hands on her hips. She probably needed to start working out herself, or she'd look as out of place among the club patrons as she'd felt the night before.

"You're not playing," Ben admonished her. "You're thinking."

Something she didn't manage very well around him, especially when he had his shirt off. "I'm trying to remember where I left my purse," she said, slipping into the role he'd chosen for her.

Passion leaped, lighting up his dark eyes. "I have it." He lifted her purse strap from her shoulder and claimed her bag.

"Yes, you do." She reached out for the brown leather, but he pulled back. "So, are you going to give it to me?"

"Oh, I'm going to give it to you," he promised. "What's my reward for keeping your purse safe?"

She pursed her lips as if considering how much he was worth. "Ten dollars?"

"You're cheap."

Smiling, she nodded. "Yes."

"How about a kiss?"

"Just a kiss?" she asked a bit breathlessly, as she stepped closer to his bare chest. To steady herself, as passion rushed through her head, getting her dizzy, she reached out, bracing a hand against his chest. His heart pounded madly beneath her palm.

"Can we stop at just a kiss?" he asked, dipping his head until his lips were only a breath from hers.

"We haven't been able to yet." She wished they could; she wished they could stop *before* the kiss. But she couldn't resist him. She rose up on tiptoe and closed the distance between them, pressing her lips to his.

He opened his mouth, deepening the kiss until he stole her breath away. His tongue mated with hers, sliding in and out of her mouth. His hands were busy, too, pushing her coat off her shoulders so it dropped to the tiled floor along with her purse. Then he slid his fingers up under her sweatshirt, over her bare rib cage.

His breath shuddered out. "You're not wearing a bra."

She wore a heavy sweatshirt and hadn't thought she needed it. His hands closed over her breasts and she trembled. "Ben…"

"Shh…you don't know my name," he reminded her as he moved his mouth across her cheek and down her throat. His tongue lapped at her throbbing pulse.

"Then what do I call you?"

"Shh…" he murmured again as he moved his hands, sliding them up and down so that his palms teased her hardened nipples.

"Ooh…"

Her moan must have broken his control because his touch got rougher, more urgent. They began to shed the rest of their clothes, and he pulled the sweatshirt over her head and then dragged her jeans down over her hips.

"You're wearing underwear," he said, tsking, as if disappointed. But his eyes flared with passion as he studied the polka-dot satin panties. He dropped his pants and the black boxers he'd worn beneath them.

Her breath shuddered out now. "Ooh…"

"Your turn," he said, hooking a thumb in the satin at her hip and dragging it down. Then he lifted her until her bottom settled onto the cold surface of the bar.

"Ben, it's freezing," she protested.

But she wasn't cold for long, not as his mouth and hands moved over her body. Heat coursed through her, burning her up as he joined her on the bar. He rolled so his back was on the cold, glossy surface and she straddled him. She rose up, then settled down…onto him, taking him deep inside her.

His hands gripped her hips, helping her ride him until they both shouted out their release. Paige collapsed onto his chest; his heart raced beneath her damp cheek.

"Wow…" She kissed his shoulder, damp with perspiration. "I wouldn't mind another round of that."

His hands skimmed over her bare back, shaking slightly as he caressed her. "I can't get enough of you, Paige."

He didn't sound pleased; he sounded resigned. Was that all they were to each other, a bad habit? When they'd started back up, with their stolen moments of passion, Paige had considered their sexual involvement light and uncomplicated. Because they trusted each other, because they knew each other, they felt safe to play these sexual games with each other. But she should have remembered nothing was ever light and uncomplicated with Ben.

"I'm worried about you," he said. "Worried about you being here."

She sighed, too tired—physically and emotionally—to argue with him. "I'm not going to be here much longer. I'm going home." To her empty bed.

She scrambled off the bar and, too vulnerable to be naked with him, slipped into her discarded clothes. But it didn't matter if she wore a parka and boots, she was still exposed to him. He had always been able to see right through her. But when she looked at him, as she did now as he pulled his clothes back on, she saw a stranger. A handsome, successful man with whom she'd lived for ten years and loved even longer, but who had never really let her get to know him the way that he knew her.

She turned away from him and walked toward the entry with the black slate floor and the long narrow couches. His shoes scraped across the floor as he followed her out. "How were you going to lock up for Sebastian?" she asked.

"I have a key."

"Of course." Sebastian would have given him one. Her brother was closer to her ex than she'd ever been. Her half brother hadn't found her until ten years ago—their dad having deserted him and his mother just as he'd deserted Paige and hers. That should have been a bond that drew them close, but even though Paige had opened her home and her heart to Sebastian, he held something of himself back from her. Just as her husband had.

Secrets. She was sick to death of them.

Ben reached around her to open the door. And as he did he leaned close enough that the morning light, streaming now through the window, illuminated his face and the spatter of blood across his cheek. She lifted her fingers to it and rubbed away the smear. "You've got blood on you."

He covered her hand with his. "There must have been some on the bar."

"Is there any on me?" she asked as she made a mental note to find out who had gotten hurt.

These were her employees now. Even though Sebastian managed them, she was ultimately responsible for them.

Ben's gaze slid over her face as thoroughly as his fingers had over her body just moments before. Her breath caught in her lungs as if he had caressed her, the way her fingers were now caressing his cheek. Touching him was never a good idea. She pulled her hand away and fisted it. Even after what they'd just done…she wanted him again. Still.

"I need to get some sleep," she murmured, protesting her own need. She could inspect the flowers later—when she had enough energy to deal with them.

"Paige…" His eyes darkened with emotion, but he said nothing more, only opened the door, so she could step into the outside stairwell first. After turning the key in the lock, she hurried ahead of him up the cement stairs to where she'd parked Sebastian's car. When she'd left earlier, with the night's deposit, he'd insisted she drive his sports car instead of walking home at the late hour.

Dread gripped her as she noticed the glass broken on the pavement beside the red BMW.

"Sebastian's going to kill me," she murmured as she stepped closer to the damaged vehicle.

The side window had been broken, and the air bag spilled out of the steering wheel—deflated now with a wooden stake protruding through it and the leather beneath it. She glanced around, but that eerie sensation had left her. No one watched her now, as they had earlier.

Perhaps they trusted that she would understand their message this time. Paige shivered as she realized that none of this had been a mistake. The voice in her head had told her the truth. She didn't belong here; it was too dangerous.

Chapter 6

The office door rattled under a pounding fist. Paige's heart skipped a beat as fear filled her. At Ben's insistence, she'd locked that door but not the one to the outside stairwell.

Why hadn't he stayed?

"Paige?" a female voice called out. "Are you all right?"

"Kate!" She sprang up from her desk and fumbled with the lock.

The detective stood outside the door, her gun clutched in her hand. But the friend stepped into the office, her eyes soft with concern. "Are you all right?"

"Fine." Now that she wasn't alone. "In fact, I'm sure I overreacted. I shouldn't have called you. You're a major case detective, and this is just a little vandalism."

"And these?" Kate asked as she gestured at the arrangement on the desk. "Granted, it's been a while since anyone has sent me flowers, but still I don't think black roses are all that romantic."

"Are you sure?" Paige teased. "The concept of romance could have changed in the many years since you've tried it. I don't remember the last time you went on a date."

"You've been divorced four years. But when's the last time you dated?"

Paige shrugged. "It's been a while," she admitted. What she and Ben did together could hardly be called dating.

"Was there a card with these ugly flowers?" Kate asked.

"It's stuck to the stake."

"Stake?" The detective shuddered. "That looks like what someone pounded into the steering wheel of your car."

"Sebastian's car," Paige corrected her, then flinched as she recalled the damage to the sports coupe. "And he's going to kill me for not protecting his pride and joy."

"I think he's going to be more concerned about you than his car," Kate said. "What does the note say?"

She released a shaky breath. "It says I'm going to get what I deserve."

"You don't deserve this, Paige," Kate said, her voice husky with emotion.

She was such a good friend—something Paige never would have suspected they would become given how they'd met. Back before Paige had joined the law firm, she'd been a public defender, representing some of the people Kate had arrested. Detective Wever hadn't appreciated that Paige had sometimes gotten the charges either reduced or thrown out.

"You're right," she agreed. Whatever she might have done wrong in her life, she had already been punished enough with all that she had lost. "I think this is just a misunderstanding. Or mistaken identity. Or something. I can't have a stalker."

"Why not?"

She gestured at herself, pointing out her baggy sweatshirt and disheveled hair. "I'm hardly stalker material."

"You're beautiful, Paige," her friend assured her. "I'm sure you have guys hitting on you all the time."

"No." Ben didn't count. "I haven't dated in forever."

"So maybe it's someone you represented," Kate suggested.

"I haven't practiced criminal law in years," Paige said. "I've mostly been doing contracts and wills. Lizzy, being the divorce lawyer, is the one who gets the threats."

"It's only been a few years since you stopped practicing criminal law," Kate said. "Even after you joined the firm, you kept doing pro bono work for the public defender's office."

"Much to your disappointment," Paige said with a smile. "You sure you didn't send me the flowers? There were times you called me a few unflattering names."

"That was before I got to know you," Kate said. "Then I understood that you were only trying to help." She narrowed her eyes in a mock glare. "Damn bleeding heart…"

Remembering the stake, Paige shuddered. "Not hardly. It's just that I know that people make mistakes." Growing up, she'd watched her mother make mistake after mistake. And she vowed she'd never become like that, desperate and dependent on a man. But then she'd fallen for Ben....

"So you have no idea who could have sent these flowers or vandalized your car?"

She shrugged. "None."

But then the voice reverberated in her head, its faint echo taunting her, *You don't belong here....*

And her shrug turned into a shudder.

"What is it?" Kate asked, as perceptive as ever. "You've thought of something."

She shook her head, unwilling to admit to hearing voices. Kate, as practical as she was perceptive, would think she was crazy. "It has to be a mistake." There really was no voice inside her head.

"The flowers were left in your office. That was no mistake, Paige. And even though it's Sebastian's car, you're the one who drove it here."

She shuddered again. "And I had a strange sensation," she confessed, "a feeling that someone was watching me."

A muscle twitched along Kate's delicate jaw. "You're being stalked, Paige."

"Then it must be some random kook."

"This feels more personal than that," Kate said. Her voice deepened with concern, and her blue eyes narrowed. "You're sure your ex isn't holding a grudge over the divorce?"

Despite all the years they'd been friends, Kate had never really met Ben. All those times, before the divorce, that Paige had asked him to join her and her friends for drinks or dinner—he'd been busy with work…and whatever else that he had never shared with her.

"Ben's not holding a grudge," Paige insisted. "He never fought the divorce. We never really ever fought." Maybe if they had, they'd still be married. But, she suspected that Ben hadn't cared enough to fight with her…or for her.

"You're lucky you never fought," Kate remarked, glancing away as if unable to meet Paige's gaze. She'd never talked about her divorce, which had happened before she and Paige had become friends.

But they were friends, and because they were, Paige felt compelled to confess, "I think it has something to do with this place."

Kate met her gaze now, her blue eyes carefully guarded. "What about this place?"

"I don't know. I just feel…I just feel that there's something *off* about it. That there's some secret about it. You mentioned it last night," Paige remembered. "You know something about this place."

Kate shrugged. "Rumors. Nothing I can prove."

"What are the rumors?"

A ragged sigh slipped through Kate's lips. "Nothing that makes any sense. Just that the club and its patrons are keeping a secret."

"You don't know what the secret is?"

"Something dangerous. Something unbelievable, but no one's ever said what it is. I thought it was some urban legend—something not worth my time to investigate." That muscle twitched along her jaw again. "But one of my best friends is being threatened. It's damn well worth my time now to launch an investigation."

"I know where to start," Paige shared. Her hand trembling, she turned the knob of the office door and stepped into the hall. Then she pointed to that heavy steel door at the end of it. "That's the key to the secret. If only I had the key to the door."

A small smile curved Kate's lips. "I seldom need keys."

Instead of excitement or anticipation, a chill of dread rushed over Paige. She wouldn't like whatever they discovered behind that door. When Kate pulled a small kit of metal tools from her pocket, Paige nearly stopped her, but then she pulled back her hand.

She hadn't fought Ben, either. She should have pushed him; she should have fought to learn all his secrets. But then, like now, she'd been afraid of what she might discover.

It was well past time to face her fears.

"Live, damn you, live," Ben beseeched the man lying atop the table. Blood gurgled around the stake protruding from Owen Buskirk's chest.

He understood how Sebastian had talked this man into protecting Paige. Buskirk owed Ben for saving the mortal he'd tried to turn and nearly killed instead. God, he'd been furious with the careless vampire for nearly killing an innocent girl. He'd threatened that if Owen ever needed him that he wouldn't help.

"Live," he pleaded with his patient as he worked frantically to repair the damage. Owen was an idiot, but he didn't deserve what had been done to him. "You have to tell me who did this to you."

Ben needed to know before the stake was driven into Paige's heart. After cutting through what was left of the guy's chest, he reached for the rib-splitter. But his efforts were futile—the heart had been splintered to pieces.

This undead had just become very dead.

"Someone's trying to open the door," a feminine voice warned him.

He glanced to Ingrid, the vampiress who occasionally served as his nurse. She hadn't even bothered helping him with this patient, as if she'd instinctively known what Ben had refused to accept.

He lifted his gaze to the monitor that displayed the images from the surveillance camera hidden in the hall. His breath backed up in his lungs as he realized it was Paige standing at the door, beside the dark-haired detective who was messing with the lock. Fear was stark on her face, which was eerily pale on the black-and-white screen.

"Oh, God," he murmured. "We need to move him." But even if they managed to get him through the only other exit and into the sewers, they wouldn't have time to clean up the blood that overflowed the metal exam table and pooled on the cement floor beneath it.

"There's no time," Ingrid said, voicing his thought aloud. "If they get inside, we will have to get rid of them."

"No! I won't let you hurt her."

"You know the rules of the secret society," Ingrid reminded him. "No mortal can know of us and live."

"You've made an exception to that rule," he pointed out.

"You're the only exception," Ingrid said, "because we need you."

"And when you don't?" Would he be expendable, too?

"We're going to need you," she said as she glanced from the body on the table back to him, "as long as we can trust you."

Ben clenched his jaw, holding back a sharp retort. Losing his temper wouldn't protect Paige.

"You're going to want us to keep trusting you," Ingrid warned him as the doorknob rattled. "And that means protecting our secret."

He focused on the monitor again, on the fear

on Paige's face and the frustration on the detective's. *Please, leave it alone. Just leave it alone...*

He had no clue if Paige would hear or heed his telepathic message. But all those other times that he'd seen the questions in her eyes, her need to know where he'd been and what he'd been doing, he'd sent her the same message. And her questions had remained in her eyes, unasked.

And the distance and distrust had grown between them.

He'd done it to protect her, as he had to protect her now.

"We need to get him out of here and leave," he urged her, "in order to protect the secret."

Ingrid gestured toward the dead vampire. "This is why mortals can't learn about our society. This is what happens when they find out about us. They set out to destroy all of us. They feel they must kill what they fear."

Ben shook his head. "You don't know that a mortal did this. I have treated more wounds that were a result of vampire violence—either to other vampires or to mortals who were hurt as a result of what a vampire had done to them."

"You shouldn't be treating the mortals."

"I'm a doctor first," he said. "I've taken an oath." Just as he'd once spoken vows to Paige, vows he would not break. He couldn't leave the Underground, not with her in danger.

He glanced to the monitor and the two women standing in the hall, then back to the knob as it turned....

Chapter 7

"What the hell—" Sebastian's heart slammed against his ribs as he ran down the hall to where Paige and her friend stood at the door.

"Sebastian," Paige said, turning toward him. She threw her arms around his neck. "I'm so sorry…."

"Sorry?" Patting her back, he stared over her head at what the detective had done to the lock. Scratches marred the steel surface, but the door remained shut. And locked?

"About your car," Paige said. She pulled back

and lifted her gaze to his, her blue eyes wide with regret. "Did you see it or have the police already taken it away?"

"Oh, yeah, my car," he said with a brief wince.

"You got my voice mail then?"

He shook his head. "No, I talked to Ben. He told me what happened."

"Where is Ben?" Kate asked, finally turning her focus away from the door to stare at Sebastian.

"He was with me," Paige said, her face flushing with color, "when we discovered the damage to your car. But then he had to rush off. He had an emergency."

"What are you two doing?" He gestured behind them.

"Something strange is going on around here," Paige said. "And Kate's going to investigate."

"Would you open this door for us?" the detective asked. "You've been managing Club Underground for a while. You must have a key."

"There's a key somewhere in the office," he admitted. "I could probably dig it out if we had a while."

"I can wait," Kate said, folding her arms across her rather impressive chest.

He shrugged. "Fine. I'm pretty tired myself. Haven't been to bed yet."

"Really?"

He chuckled. "Well, I haven't been to sleep yet. I doubt Paige has, either. And don't you work nights, Detective?"

"So what are you suggesting?" Kate asked. "That we all sleep on this? Why would that be necessary if you have nothing to hide?"

The woman was too damn smart, and that made her a danger—to him and herself.

"It's really not a problem," he said. "I'll dig out the key and open it." He glanced up, at the camera hidden behind a heat duct register, and wished he could see inside the secret room.

He hoped like hell his vampire friend had been saved and they'd all slipped out the other exit as he stepped inside the office. After banging the desk drawers open and closed a few times, he rejoined the women who had not budged from their spot. He pulled out the ring of keys he always carried. "I think it was right here all along," he said with a forced laugh. "Per the fire department ordinance, I'm supposed to carry it with me all the time since it opens up the other exit from the club."

"Other exit?" Paige asked. "But you said nothing was behind that door."

"Yeah, I didn't want to mention what it really was, or I thought that you might not want to invest in the club," he admitted. Honestly.

He had kept a lot from her—ever since he'd entered her life again. But, without her money, the building manager would have shut down the club. Ben had been unable to save the last owner, who'd been fatally wounded in a fight in the club. Sebastian couldn't have asked Ben for the money; he'd already asked too much of him, forcing him to keep secrets that had cost him his marriage. And with nowhere else to go in Zantrax, most of the society would have moved away—to more welcoming cities and eras. Sebastian hadn't wanted to leave her.

But she would have been safer had he left.

"Why wouldn't you want to mention another exit?" Paige asked, her blond brows furrowed in confusion.

"Because it's an exit to be used only when the other one is blocked. It goes into the sewers," he said.

"Sewers?" Paige asked, her nose wrinkling with distaste.

"It's the only other way out of a basement club. So you ladies might want to step to the side of the hall in case some rats run out when I open the door."

Paige clutched at the sleeve of his suit jacket. "Rats?"

He slid the key into the lock. As he did, Paige dropped her hand from his arm and moved behind him. Kate, however, stepped closer. And covered his hand with hers.

"Uh, that's okay," she said. "You don't need to open it. I can see now that this would open into the sewers."

"Well, there's actually another door behind it," he admitted, "to the stairwell, which takes you down deeper into the sewer. Then you have to follow that tunnel to the ladder that leads up to a manhole cover in the street."

All of which was true. Zantrax sewers were legendary as passageways for those who wanted to remain unseen. And undead. Club Underground bridged the world between mortals and immortals. A bridge that few should dare to cross.

"Are you sure you don't want me to open it?" he asked, turning the key in the lock.

The detective tightened her grasp on his hand. "No, it's not necessary." She was clever and perceptive. "As you said earlier, it's late. You should take Paige home."

It was too late for that. The sun was just rising as he'd slipped inside the club moments earlier. "I can't," he said. "Can you see her home? Make sure she gets there safely?"

"But you said you were tired," Kate reminded him. "Aren't you going home? So that you can stay with her?"

"Just because I'm going to bed doesn't mean I'm going home," he teased with a wink at the obviously disapproving detective. "Besides which, she'll be safer with you. You carry a gun."

"I don't need anyone to see me home," Paige said, her chin lifted with pride and independence.

He suppressed a grimace over his pang of guilt and regret. Ben was right—he shouldn't have involved her at all. She should have been the one coming to him for help—not the other way around—but he'd never been there for her like she deserved. She deserved so much better than to have him in her life…

"You don't have a car, remember?" he called after her.

"Neither do you," Kate reminded him with a faint smile.

He forced his cocky grin and stepped closer to the sexy detective. "But I never have a problem getting a ride."

"You're wasting your time flirting with me, Sebastian," she warned him.

He only flirted with her because he knew she'd never take him up on his many offers. It wouldn't take a woman like her long to learn everything.

"I'm too much for you to handle, Detective," he teased.

She laughed but didn't deny it. "I already have more than I can handle, Sebastian." She turned to Paige, who'd stepped out of the office clutching her purse. Instead of joining them where they stood at the door, she headed off down the hall. "But the most important thing is to find who's stalking your sister."

"No," he said.

She glanced at him in surprise.

"The most important thing is to keep her safe."

Kate opened her mouth, as if she had questions for him. But then she only nodded and headed after her friend.

Sebastian leaned back against the steel door and exhaled a ragged sigh of relief. Then the metal creaked and the door opened. He shifted his weight forward and turned, so that he wouldn't fall into the room.

God, he hated that room—hated the smell of death that clung to it. Ben had saved many people, himself included, but he'd lost many, too. Like the man who lay atop the table, the stake protruding from his chest.

This was Sebastian's fault, too. He'd called in a favor to have Owen protect Paige—and the man had died carrying it out. Guilt and self-condemnation gripped him, tightening the muscles in his stomach.

Condemnation filled Ingrid's dark eyes, for a moment crowding out the madness, as she met his gaze. "You've done it again, Sebastian."

"I stopped them from entering," he said, and he stopped himself now, holding back from crossing that threshold into the room of death. Blood stained the floor beneath Ben's makeshift operating table. The surgeon was gone, but he'd been there, trying to save another patient.

"Those mortals wouldn't have even been here if not for you," Ingrid persisted.

"No," he agreed. "None of them would have, including Ben."

"Who is she—this new mistress of the Underground?" Ingrid asked, her usually husky voice even thicker with disdain.

"Someone important to me," he said. "I don't want her getting hurt. If you know who's threatening her…" Or if she were the one threatening her…

Ingrid's hatred of humans was well known. "And if I did…?"

"You'd be wise to let them know that I'm going to stop them," Sebastian said.

"Stop them?" Her dark eyes widened with curiosity and amusement. "How?"

He glanced over her shoulder, to the body with the stake through the heart. "I will do whatever necessary to protect her."

"So she is important to you," Ingrid said. "She's not your sister, as she thinks. Who is she really?"

"She's my daughter."

* * *

Frustration nagged at Paige as she jammed the key into the lock and opened the door…to her condo. She shuddered at the thought of opening that *other* door and having rats run out.

Maybe it was better that she didn't learn whatever made her feel unwelcome—and out of place—at Club Underground. Catching sight of her reflection in the mirror above the hall table, she winced at the dark circles beneath her eyes and the lines fanning them and her mouth. She looked like her mother, not just because of her blond hair and fair skin, but because she looked older than she actually was—courtesy of all the stress and pain she'd had in her life. "Forty's the new thirty, my ass."

Her age was probably why she felt so out of place at Club Underground. Everyone else, patrons and staff, including Sebastian, seemed so much younger and more beautiful. Kate was wrong; no one was stalking Paige. No one would want to….

Then she tilted her head, listening…to the sound of running water. The walls were thick in the old warehouse that had been converted to condos; the noise could not be coming from an adjoining unit. It had to be coming from her bathroom. Her pulse raced with fear. She should have had Kate walk her to the door, as the detective had wanted. But Paige had insisted that no one would have gotten past the doorman in the lobby or her security system.

She glanced to the alarm panel near the door. The lights were off; someone had already disabled it. How? Only she and Sebastian knew the code, and he'd remained back at the club.

She fumbled inside her purse for her cell phone. She could call Kate again; she might not have left the parking lot yet. But why would someone break in to use her bathroom?

She dropped her purse onto the hall table and reached instead for one of the bottles on the wine rack beneath it. As she had back at the club, she intended to use it as a weapon. She lifted it, like a bat, over her shoulder as she stepped inside her bedroom. When she crossed the hardwood floor to the open bathroom doorway, the water sputtered and cut off. Steam billowed from the room.

Paige tightened her grip on her weapon of choice. Her intruder would need another shower after she broke the bottle over his head.

But then the man stepped out, water sluicing over his naked skin—all that naked skin. And she dropped the bottle onto the floor. The neck spun until the cork pointed toward him.

"So today's game is spin the bottle?" Ben asked.

"Game?" she repeated, her eyes wide as her gaze traveled up and down his body.

Ben tensed, every muscle taut with desire at her blatant interest in him. He would have figured he was too worried—and too tired—to want her again. But none of that mattered now. He would want her even if he was dead, which since he'd learned of the secret society had become an inevitable fate.

"Is this a game," she asked, "your breaking in here and scaring me *again?*"

"I didn't break in." But had it been necessary he would have, so that he'd been able to secure the place before she'd come home.

"Sebastian's not here," she said. "He didn't let you in."

"He didn't need to," he explained. "He gave me a key."

"He gave you a key?" she repeated. "To my place? And he gave you the security code, too?"

"I guessed the security code."

Color flushed her face, making her blue eyes even brighter. "It…it's just easier to remember," she sputtered.

While she was embarrassed that she'd used the date of their wedding as the code, like they had at the home they'd shared, Ben was encouraged that there might be hope for them. At least he had been until he reminded himself that he had nothing to offer her but secrets and danger.

"Of course," he agreed, "it's easy to remember."

"So you just let yourself in," she remarked, then gestured toward the bathroom, "and helped yourself to my shower?"

"I needed it." He'd needed to rid himself of the blood and the scent of death that always clung to him when he went to the Underground.

"Why didn't you use the showers in the locker room?"

He turned away and reached for a towel. He ran the terry cloth across his skin before wrapping it around his waist. "Locker room?"

"At the hospital. You had to leave me at the club to treat a patient, right?"

He hadn't given her much of an explanation

when he'd had her lock herself inside the office to wait for the detective. But while she'd been looking at the damage to Sebastian's car, he had seen the mortally wounded vampire and had known someone needed him more than she had.

"Your patient is stable now?" she asked with her usual concern and compassion.

He flinched and shut his eyes on the image of Owen lying there with his chest open, the stake protruding from his savaged heart. "I wouldn't say that...."

"Then you should go back to the hospital," she urged him, "and take care of your patient."

"There's nothing more I can do for him," he said with a sigh. The society of undead buried their own dead. "I wanted to get back to you...to make sure that you're all right."

"I'm fine."

"I wish I believed you," he said, "but you don't look fine, Paige."

She lifted a hand to her face. "I got caught in the rain."

He glanced around her to the bedroom window; rain ran in rivulets down the glass, but the sky had lightened as there were only a few gray clouds. As always, he breathed a small sigh of relief during the day. The undead didn't need him then—unless they'd been out in the sunlight. But the undead were not his only patients; he had other ones—human patients at the hospital, to which he'd often been called away from Paige.

"You should get out of your wet clothes," he suggested, intent on taking advantage of the time he had with her.

Her lips lifted in a faint smile. "Are you trying to get me naked?"

Even with clothes on, she was naked to him, her face vulnerable as it revealed all her feelings. All her pain and fear.

His heart contracted with regret for what his secrets had cost them both. "I came here to make sure you're all right."

She turned away from him, toward the window that the rain sluiced down as it had his skin earlier in the shower. "And I told you I'm fine. I reported the vandalism. I have a detective working on the case now. I've done everything I was supposed to do."

Now he suspected she was talking about something else—something they had never talked about.

"I know," he assured her.

She shook her head. "No. No, you don't. You don't know me, and I don't know you."

"We're playing that game again?" he asked. "Strangers?"

"We're not playing," she said with a slight edge, but then she sighed and shook her head. "You're a burglar, and I'm the homeowner who found you in my shower."

He hated the games, hated more that they actually weren't playing at being strangers. But if playing the game was the only way he could stick close to her, he'd play....

He would do anything to protect her—even let her go, if he had to...

Chapter 8

Warm lips brushed the nape of Paige's neck, beneath the swing of her high ponytail. "You should have joined me in the shower."

She shivered at his touch, or maybe she was just cold because the rain had left her sweatshirt damp, her skin chilled. "I don't shower with strange men," she told him.

The lips lingered, nibbling at the skin above her leaping pulse before curving into a smile. "So I'm not just a stranger, I'm strange, too?"

"Yes." Even more so than when they'd been

married. "I have no idea where you go—when you just suddenly leave me. Sebastian said the hospital, and I've always assumed that's where. But you've never really told me."

He tensed. "When we were married, did you think I was cheating on you?"

"I'm a lawyer." Was a lawyer. "At a firm with divorce lawyers…" But it wasn't just because of her career that she was cynical. She'd lived through all her mother's heartaches over picking the wrong men, men who'd used and left her over and over again. God, she had become her mother.

His arms tightened around her waist, his fingers biting into her flesh. "I never—*never*—cheated on you, Paige, and I never would."

"We're not married," she reminded him. She couldn't expect him to be faithful to her. If only he could be open with her.

"Just remember, Paige, that I always come back to—"

She turned in his arms and swallowed his words with her mouth. She didn't want declarations or promises he'd never be able to keep. She just wanted him. Linking their fingers, she pulled Ben along with her, her lips clinging to his as they stumbled a few short steps to the bed.

The back of her knees hit the edge of the mattress and she tumbled down, alone, onto the rumpled blankets.

Ben stood above her, clad only in that towel tucked around his thin waist. She wriggled out of her jeans, kicking them down her legs. Then she pulled the damp sweatshirt over her head, baring her breasts. Ben's dark eyes flared with passion as he stared down at her.

She ran her fingertips from her throat over the curve of one breast to the elastic holding her polka-dot satin panties up.

Something rose beneath his towel, tenting the terry cloth. He groaned, "Paige…"

Leaving the hand at the edge of her panties, she lifted her other one to her mouth, licking her fingers. Ben's nostrils flared as his breathing grew harsh. His voice rough, he admonished her, "You're bad…"

With one last lick, she took her fingers from her mouth and slid them down her body again. This time she didn't skim over her breast, she cupped it, then ran her wet fingertip across her nipple, which peaked beneath her touch.

Her breathing caught as pleasure streaked through her. "Oh…"

"You're *very* bad…" His towel dropped, pulled free of his waist by his jutting erection.

Her other hand edged farther beneath the satin, her fingers stroking over the curls visible beneath the thin polka-dot fabric. Then she parted herself, sliding first one finger, then two, into her damp heat.

"Ooh…" she moaned again, rising slightly off the edge of her mattress. She gazed up at him, beseeching him to help her, "Ben…"

He shook his head. "You don't need me." Sadness and regret darkened his eyes. "You don't…"

She started to withdraw her hand, but he shouted at her, "Don't!" Then he lowered his voice, and his body, onto the mattress beside her, "Don't stop…"

His hand covered the one at her breast, moving her fingers so that she plucked at her distended nipple. Then his mouth settled onto her other breast, pressing kisses to the swollen flesh before his lips closed over the nipple.

"Don't stop," he murmured, licking her areole, then teasing her nipple with just the tip of his tongue.

She shuddered and slid the fingers back in. He reached down with his free hand, above the satin, closing over hers beneath, driving her fingers deeper inside her, grinding her palm against her clit until she came. Tears streaked from the corners of her eyes, falling onto the rumpled sheets.

"Ben…"

He lifted his mouth from her breast, then pulled her hand from her panties. He drew each wet finger into his mouth, lapping and licking. Then he reached down again and jerked at the satin until the panties tore free of her hips.

Before she could reach for him, he rolled off the bed and knelt at the side of the mattress. Then he pulled her to the edge, so that her legs dangled off the high bed, just above the floor.

"My turn," he said, his voice hoarse. He licked his way from her knees, up the inside of her thighs, watching her as she propped herself on her elbows.

"Ben…"

"Touch yourself again," he ordered her. "Touch your breasts, imagine my mouth on them, wet and hungry…."

"You're awfully bossy for an intruder," she teased.

"I may be dangerous," he said. "So you better do what I say…."

He was definitely dangerous—to her heart. But she couldn't resist him. She settled back onto the mattress and reached for her nipples, rolling them between her fingertips. Then his mouth moved between her legs, his tongue dipping into her heat. He pushed her legs farther apart as he devoured her. Hungrily.

Her fingers trembled as she continued to play with her breasts. Pleasure arched her back, raising her from the mattress, as he pulled her tight against his mouth, his tongue delving deep, then pulling out to lap at her clit.

She wept as he teased her, pleading with him for more. But he took his time, savoring her with every lick, every soft bite of his hungry mouth. Finally he drove deep, with his tongue, while his hands skimmed up her body and covered hers on her breasts.

She convulsed, as a powerful orgasm shuddered through her. "Ben..." she sobbed.

But he pulled back, replacing his tongue with his throbbing cock, pushing the thick, long length of his erection into her wetness. Her muscles squeezed him, trying to hold him, as he withdrew, then slammed back into her.

Again and again.

She arched off the bed, meeting his every thrust. More orgasms tore through her until he stiffened, then cried out. Heat filled her as he came. Then he pulled free, collapsing onto the bed next to her.

She rolled to her side, overwhelmed. But he remained facedown on the mattress, his body jerking with each harsh breath he dragged into his lungs.

"Ben…"

He turned toward her. "You're going to kill me, you know. Brilliant cardiologist suffers heart attack while making love…."

"I don't know about that," she mused.

His body tensed for a moment, as if he thought she didn't consider what they did making love. Only sex.

So she lifted a brow and teased, "You consider yourself brilliant? Really?"

He reared up and leaned over her, nipping at her sensitive nipple with his teeth, as he pushed his thumb inside her, strumming her clit as he might a guitar. Except that Ben wasn't musical. Just brilliant at making her come.

She tensed, then broke apart, coming again. She bit his shoulder, hard, in protest at how easily he controlled her body. His teeth closed over her nipple, nipping.

She rose up, coming again. "Oh, Ben!"

"You can't deny my brilliance now," he teased her.

She knew he was kidding because Ben had never had an ego, just a hard work ethic. And a hard dick, which pulsed at her hip. She closed her hand around him, holding his hot, pulsing flesh. He groaned again but pulled her hand away.

"We have to discuss something."

She hated how this was straying into a serious conversation she'd rather avoid. She sat up and swung her legs over the edge of the mattress.

"I'm worried about you, Paige," he said, "about this crazy stalker." His hands closed over her shoulders, turning her to face him. "I think I should move in here."

Her heart knocked against her ribs. "What?"

"Or you can move in with me," he offered, his dark eyes earnest.

"Ben!"

He sighed. "It would only have to be until the stalker is caught, Paige. You're not safe here alone."

"I'm not alone," she pointed out. "Sebastian lives here, too."

"Casanova?" he scoffed. "How much time does he really spend here?"

"Not much," she admitted. "But I'm fine alone. You don't need to worry about me."

"But I do." His throat moved as he swallowed hard. "Even before you picked up a stalker, I worried about you."

"Ben, I take care of myself," she reminded him, resenting that she had to. "I always have."

"I know." His brown eyes grew soft and wistful. "But I wish…"

"What?"

"I wish I had taken care of you when we were married," he admitted.

She laughed at his thought of chivalry. "I didn't let you." If only she'd taken his advice…

"But I should have tried," he insisted, his fingers clenching her shoulders. "I should have been there for you more."

She shook her head, suddenly weary from more than making love. "That's all in the past, Ben, and it doesn't matter. We're not married anymore."

His eyes darkened with emotion. "What are we, Paige?"

She tried to pull out of his arms, but he held her tight, his fingers biting into her skin. "I don't know, Ben."

She didn't have an answer for him or herself.

"We're not married," he agreed. "We're not really dating. We don't go out to dinner or a movie."

"Who does that?" she asked. "We never went out to dinner or a movie." They'd always been too tired from working such long, hard hours. Or he hadn't been around. He'd been around for so little of their marriage.

"I don't know." He shrugged. "Maybe we should have...."

She smiled, amused that he would think they *could* have. Neither of them was much made for leisure activities...except making love. "We were never *those* people, Ben, not when we first started going out or when we were married."

"What people?"

"You know the ones, the couple who hold hands while they walk around the mall, the ones who stare into each other's eyes over a candlelit dinner."

His eyes softened with regret, as if he wished they had been. "Paige..."

They both carried too much regret. None of it could change what had happened between them, what had gone wrong.

"It's okay," she assured him. "We never had time to be *those* people. I was busy, too." Not as busy as he'd been, but she'd submerged herself in her work, too.

At first, because she'd been determined to be exactly the opposite of her mother. But then she'd fallen for Ben. And she'd still worked too much, so that she wouldn't notice how little he'd been there.

"We should have made time," Ben said.

"It's too late now," she said again.

He shook his head, obviously unwilling to accept the finality. "It's *never* too late."

"We can't change the past," Paige insisted.

"No, we can't," he agreed. "But I can be here for you now. I can protect you, Paige."

"You might be able to protect me from my stalker," she said, "if I have one. But who will protect me from you?"

A muscle twitched in his cheek. But he didn't profess his undying love or the fact that he'd never hurt her. They both knew he couldn't promise her those things.

"We can't change the past," she said as she drew in a shaky breath. "And we can't change the fact that we have no future."

He'd already accepted that they had no future. If only he'd realized it sooner and let her go… then maybe she wouldn't be in danger now.

"We don't have a future together," he agreed, but hated himself for the pain that darkened her usually bright eyes. "But we need to make sure *you* have a future. I need to move in here, so that I can protect you from physical harm." As she'd already pointed out, he was the last one who could protect her from emotional harm. "And you need to stop going to the club. It's not safe for you there."

Her eyes crinkled at the corners as the sadness left them, and she laughed.

"I'm serious, Paige."

"You're deluded," she retorted. "I may let you tell me what to do there—" she pointed to the rumpled bed "—but only there. You're not my husband anymore. You can't tell me how to live my life."

Frustration had his temper snapping and he bitterly remarked, "We both know I've never been able to tell you what to do."

As the hurt and guilt flashed in her eyes, he wished the words back. It wasn't her fault. It was his. He was the medical expert—the friggin' world-renowned and otherworld renowned cardiologist. He should have known.

Pride and anger replaced the hurt in her narrowed eyes. "No, you'd actually have to be around in order to tell me what to do," she said, the smile leaving her face as bitterness sharpened her voice. "And you weren't around for much of our marriage."

He couldn't argue with her, nor could he apologize—not without offering an explanation that would put her in more danger than she already was.

"Why are you around now, Ben?" she asked.

Guilt. Fear. Love. He could have named any of them and been speaking the truth. But then he'd have to explain something that defied explanation. The damn secret society.

"I'm worried about you," he said. "You're in danger."

She shook her head. "You don't know that…."

"The flowers, the car…"

"That all could have been a mistake," she insisted stubbornly.

How had he forgotten how stubborn Paige could be? It was one of the things he loved about her. "*You* can't take that chance. And neither can I," he said. "Let me move in here. Let me take care of you."

She laughed again, but this time tears sparkled in her eyes. "Oh, Ben, that would only set us both up for disappointment."

"What do you mean?" If she was worried about him falling for her again, it was already too late. He had never fallen out of love with her, and he worried that he never would—no matter that they had no future.

"You keep leaving," she reminded him. "You just take off, with no warning, with no explanation of where you're going or where you've been."

"I'm a doctor, Paige," he said. "You knew that when you married me. You knew I'd work long hours and be on call twenty-four seven."

She shook her head. "Maybe when you were an intern you needed to work those crazy hours. But not now."

"I have patients. I have a responsibility to them." No matter *what* they were.

"What about us?"

He flinched. "I know, Paige. I wasn't there for you…like I should have been."

"And you can't promise that it'll be different now," she pointed out.

Despite all his secrets, she really knew him too well. "No," he admitted with a heavy sigh.

"You can't protect me if you're not here."

"I'll be here," he vowed. "I'll stick close to you."

She shook her head. "Don't make a promise you've never been able to keep."

He pushed a hand through his still-damp hair and sighed. Damn it to hell, but she was right, as usual. It was another of her traits that had charmed as much as it had annoyed him.

"You always leave me," she reminded him, the tears overflowing her eyes to trail down her face like the rain on the window. "So do what you do best…leave."

He sucked in a breath of pain over her resolute rejection. "Paige?"

"And this time, don't come back," she said. "I can't keep doing this."

"But playing these games was your idea," he reminded her, with a flash of anger.

He had tried to do the right thing; he'd tried to

stay away from her after the divorce. But after a few months of no contact, she'd starting coming to him. A blow job at his office. A quickie in the backseat of his SUV. She'd shown up sporadically, weeks or sometimes months passing before she came to him again. And so desperate to see her, to touch her, to taste her, he'd started coming to her.

"It was a mistake," she said, "to think that we could keep it light and unemotional. We've never been about fun and games." She released a shuddery breath. "We're all about secrets and pain."

"I'm sorry." Not just about the pain he'd caused her...but the pain she would not let him protect her from.

Paige held back her tears until the door closed behind Ben. But then, instead of shedding them, she blinked them away. She'd cried enough over him.

Her body hummed with the pleasure he'd given her—again and again. And over the past four years, she'd kept seeking him out for more. She hadn't imagined the pleasure only he could give her, but she had forgotten the subsequent pain.

She couldn't move on with her life if she kept him in her life. Even if she was really in danger, he couldn't protect her. He could only cause her more pain, just as she had caused him.

Her heart contracted as she remembered the look on his face—the raw pain of her rejection. He hadn't looked that upset even when she'd divorced him. In fact, she'd often thought that he'd looked more relieved than hurt when she'd served him with papers.

He hadn't been relieved tonight. She wouldn't kid herself that it was because he loved her. He had agreed with everything she'd said and was acting more out of obligation than love.

But it was time she protected herself. And she couldn't do that by hiding away. That little voice in her head might be convinced she didn't belong at Club Underground, but Paige was not.

At the moment, she had nowhere else to go.

Chapter 9

Ben expelled a breath but hesitated before drawing in another. He hated the smell of this place. The stench of the blood, the death, the sewer…

Sebastian shuddered. "Why'd we have to talk here?"

"Paige can't see us together," Ben said.

And she was out there, just beyond the steel door, down the hall in her office. The club had closed for the night; all the patrons had left but she had yet to go home. God, she was stubborn.

"Why not?" Sebastian asked. "I can't talk to my *ex-brother-in-law?*"

Ben shook his head. "Not now. She'll know what we're talking about."

"What are we talking about?" Sebastian asked.

"Her," Ben replied. "You have to stick close to her. She won't let me."

Because she wanted nothing to do with him anymore. She wouldn't take his calls or return his messages except to leave one of her own. *I don't want to see you. Or talk to you anymore. Please leave me alone....*

He'd erased the message, but he would never forget the words—or the conviction in her voice. She'd been hurt and confused when she'd served him with divorce papers. She wasn't confused anymore; she was certain she didn't want him in her life.

"She won't let me protect her, either," Sebastian admitted with a heavy sigh. "It doesn't matter if she sees us together or not. She keeps accusing me of hovering. She insists she's not in any danger."

"We both know better."

Sebastian sighed again. "And so does everyone else. After Owen's murder, I can't convince anyone else to help me keep an eye on her."

Ben shrugged. "It doesn't matter. We can't trust anyone else. *You* have to protect her."

"But I don't know—"

"This is your mess. You brought me into this," Ben reminded him, frustration gripping him as he remembered the first time he'd seen this room. With the young man he'd believed his brother-in-law bleeding to death on the table, a stake protruding from his heart. "You brought *her* into this—you brought her into the world."

And he had broken the law of the secret society when he had. Vampires were not supposed to procreate with mortals; they weren't supposed to mate with them, either. But that was a law too many of the undead had broken for it ever to be steadfastly enforced.

Sebastian's eyes glistened with regret and love. "She can never know that...."

"That you're her dad instead of her younger half brother?" A claim she had too readily accepted as fact when Sebastian had showed up at their door ten years ago. "Yeah, that would kind of blow the damn secret out of the water."

"And if she learns it..."

"If..." Ben snorted. "Does it matter? She doesn't know it now, but she's already in danger."

"Is she?" the other man asked. "It's been over a week and nothing else has happened."

"Someone is threatening her," Ben reminded him.

Maybe it was time he threatened back. He'd already lost Paige once because of the damn secret. He didn't intend to lose her completely.

But then a scream penetrated the metal door, the voice shrill with terror. And terrifyingly familiar. Paige.

Was it already too late?

Paige pressed a trembling hand against her throat, where blood oozed between her fingers. With her other hand she fumbled for the light switch in her dark office. Before she could find it, the lamp flickered on her desk, and the faint glow of the bulb penetrated the shattered green shade and illuminated the trashed room.

She lurched to her feet and stumbled over the legs of the chair she'd thrown. Keeping that hand pressed against her wound, she tossed aside files and books as she looked for her purse and cell phone. Like the chair, the purse was upended—its contents spilled. She needed to get a purse with a damn zipper. Spying the glint of metal beneath the desk, she reached for the phone just as strong hands closed around her shoulders.

Thrusting her elbow back, she writhed and fought to free herself again from her assailant. "Let me go!"

"Paige, shh…it's me," a familiar deep voice assured her as he turned her to face him.

"Ben!" She threw her arms around his neck and clung to him. She'd never been so happy that he hadn't listened to her and stayed away.

His hands trembling on her shoulders, he pulled her back. His dark eyes widened, and all the color drained from his handsome face. "You're hurt! You're bleeding…." His fingertips gently probed the wound.

"It's just a scratch," she assured him, feeling as if he needed more comfort than she did now.

His breath shuddered out. "It's not deep, but I should take you to—"

"The hospital," Sebastian interjected as he dropped onto his knees beside them. "You should take her to the hospital…if she needs stitches."

She shook her head as she pushed aside Ben's fingers and touched the wound. "It's not bleeding much now."

"I need to clean and dress it," Ben said, his jaw taut. "Let's get you to the E.R."

She glanced back to her cell phone. "I need to call the police first."

"What happened, Paige?" Sebastian asked.

She shivered. "I don't know. It all happened so fast. One minute I was doing paperwork. The next it was dark and someone grabbed me."

"You fought," Ben said, his voice gruff with satisfaction and surprise.

He had every reason to be surprised. Until a week ago in her condo, she had never really fought with him. Or for him.

She nodded and wished she had fought before.

"Did you see who attacked you?" he asked, his hands tightening on her shoulders.

"No." She trembled now, but with anger, not fear, over the way she'd been ambushed in the dark. "I couldn't see anything."

But she'd heard the voice, this time outside her head, in a whisper so raspy she'd been unable to tell if it was feminine or masculine. She shuddered now as she remembered the warmth of the breath against her neck as she'd been told again, "You don't belong here...."

Bracing her hands on Ben's shoulders, she levered herself to her feet. But as soon as she stood, she swayed. Dizziness lightened her head and dimmed her vision. She drew in a steadying breath, but before she could regain her balance, Ben swung her up in his arms.

"I'm fine," she said, even though she couldn't stop trembling now that she'd started.

"No, you're not," Ben said. "I'm taking you to the hospital."

"I need to call the police," she insisted.

"You can call your friend from the hospital," he said as he carried her down the hall.

"Where did you come from?" she asked. "You and Sebastian?"

"We were out here, at the bar," her brother answered. "We were having a drink."

She glanced toward the bar, but no glasses sat atop the shiny granite surface. Would they have washed them before responding to her screams? She doubted it. "If you were out here, in the light, you would have seen who it was," she pointed out. "Who attacked me?"

A muscle twitched in his jaw as Ben shook his head. "We didn't see anything, Paige. We only heard your screams."

"I'll bring your car around," Sebastian offered, running out the door ahead of them.

When he was gone, Paige focused on her ex-husband. "Where were you, Ben?" she asked. The question was one she had wanted to ask him so many times before. But she'd been afraid of the answer—afraid that he might have been cheating on her.

"I told you I'd be here for you," he reminded her.

Like so many times before, over the years, he hadn't really answered her question. And he hadn't kept her safe.

Ben stared at the undead who had responded to his summons and gathered at Club Underground just hours after the attack. Instead of seeing them, he saw Paige's face—her skin pale but for the blood streaking from the wound on her throat. He recognized the mark, but fortunately only one fang had broken her skin. But if it had nicked an artery…

She wouldn't have been able to fight off her attacker. There would have been no screams for him and Sebastian to hear. No warning of her impending death.

He forced that image from his mind, unwilling to contemplate the horror of it. Instead, he focused on the horror before him. They didn't look like monsters; they looked like movie stars: beautiful, sexy and eternally young. But he'd seen some of the things they had done to one another and to mortals. He, more than anyone else, knew what they were capable of.

"So what's up, Doc?" Cooper West asked with a grin. He was like Sebastian—not a monster but a playboy. Still, he'd made mistakes…like Ben was beginning to believe this meeting had been a mistake. "Why'd you call us all here?"

Now it was time they learned what he was capable of—to what extremes he'd go in order to protect the woman he loved.

"Things have been happening around here," he began. "The new owner of Club Underground has been receiving threats."

"Because she doesn't belong here," a feminine voice murmured.

He glanced to Ingrid, but she sat silently, staring up at him with those dark, crazy eyes. "She owns this club now."

"But she'll never be the mistress of the Underground," another voice murmured.

"Sebastian never should have let her buy the club," Cooper said with regret.

"Well, if anyone harms Paige—again—I'm out!" Ben said as resentment fueled his rage.

"What do you mean?" someone asked.

"You can't!" A chorus of variations of the protest rang out.

Cooper shook his blond head. "You're the only one who can provide us medical treatment now."

They'd had another doctor once, but he'd proved unworthy of the trust they'd put in him.

"Of course, Sebastian has broken more hearts than you've mended, Doc," Cooper observed with a chuckle. Happily settled now, his playboy past behind him, Cooper was just amused and a little mocking that his friend still lived his old lifestyle. "Where is he?"

"At the hospital…"

Gasps emanated from the group.

"…with Paige," he continued. "Someone attacked her again tonight. There are fang marks on her throat." He slammed his fist onto the bar. The members of the society flinched, probably not over his anger but over the damage his gesture could have inflicted on one of the instruments of his special power. "This has got to stop! Now!"

"So you think one of us is threatening her?" someone asked.

He sighed. "If not one of you personally, then one of you must know who is."

"Besides what happened tonight, what were the other threats?" Cooper asked.

Ben chronicled everything that had happened, then added, "The stakes, the bite tonight... whoever's doing this is risking her discovering the secret. She's going to catch on."

"Then you know what has to happen to her," Ingrid said, the madness bright in her dark eyes.

"If Paige learns the secret, none of you will be harmed," he promised. "And I will continue to provide medical treatment. Nothing will change—as long as she doesn't get hurt."

"So you're the one with the threats now," Ingrid observed. "And you're not in a position to issue any ultimatums to us."

The hair rose on Ben's nape at the ominous tone of her husky voice. Ingrid, alone, wouldn't have concerned him, but he noted the nods of agreement from other vampires.

In calling them together, he'd acted on his

rage—not his common sense. Because if he'd been thinking clearly, he would have realized how dangerous it was to be the sole mortal in the secret society.

He'd seen the atrocities some of them had done—to one another and to hapless mortals. Was he about to experience it personally?

"Where's Ben?" Paige asked as she struggled to hold up her lids. Maybe Renae had given her a sedative, or at least something that had numbed Paige from feeling the pain of the stitches that had closed the wound on her neck.

A muscle twitched along Sebastian's cheek. "He had to leave. He had to…see a patient," Sebastian explained. Or lied on Ben's behalf.

"Why did he have to *leave* then?" she asked. "Isn't his patient here in the hospital?" Ben didn't keep regular office hours; as a surgeon, he primarily worked out of Zantrax Memorial Hospital. The only office he used, besides the O.R., was a private suite on one of the floors of the hospital.

Sebastian nodded. "Yeah, he's probably around here somewhere."

"That's good," Kate said from where she

stood next to the gurney on which Paige lay, a curtain separating her from the other patients in the E.R. "I'll have him paged, then, since I have some questions for him."

"I can answer them," Sebastian offered. "I was there with him tonight…when we heard Paige's screams."

She flinched, her throat burning as she relived those terrifying moments—crying out in fear and desperation. She'd thought no one would hear her.

"You both were there?" Kate asked. "He was never out of your sight?"

"No," Sebastian claimed. "We were having a drink at the bar."

Paige bit her lip so that she wouldn't call her brother on his lie. While Kate was her friend now, she'd always been a detective first and foremost. It was bad enough that Detective Wever had suspicions about Ben; Sebastian didn't need to get added to her suspect list.

"I don't have questions just about tonight," Kate clarified. "I want to question him about how he happened to be with Paige the last time… when the vehicle was vandalized. And wasn't he also at the club the night the flowers were left in her office?"

Sebastian shook his head. "You're wrong about Ben."

"Oh, I don't think so," Kate said.

"You don't need to interview him, Kate," Paige finally said, struggling to clear her vision and her mind. "I know he'd never hurt me."

"He wouldn't?" She arched a dark brow in apparent skepticism. "He hasn't?"

"Not intentionally," Paige insisted.

Kate shrugged, obviously unconvinced. "I'm going to see about getting him paged."

As soon as the detective slipped around the curtain, Sebastian leaned over the steel railing of the gurney. "You believe that, right? That Ben has never meant to hurt you."

She nodded. "Of course. But I have been hurt…." She touched her fingers to the gauze taped to her throat, but this was not the wound Ben had inflicted. That wound was on her heart.

"He regrets that," Sebastian claimed. "He would do anything to protect you…even risk his own life."

"What are you telling me?" The adrenaline that pumped through her veins chased away the effects of whatever drug Renae had given her. "Is Ben in danger?"

A muscle twitched along Sebastian's tightly clenched jaw as he nodded. "I'm afraid that he is."

Chapter 10

Ben winced as he eased out of the driver's seat of his Escalade. Pain radiated from his bruised ribs, echoing the pounding at his temples. He hadn't been attacked during the meeting, as he'd momentarily feared. Instead, he'd been attacked as Paige had been—in the dark. As he'd been ascending the stairs to the street, someone had stepped out of the predawn gloom and knocked him down the steps.

By the time he'd made it back to the hospital, Paige had already been checked out. Sebastian had assured Ben that she was home—safe and sound. Since the sun had risen, he believed that she was safe—for the moment. So he could sleep without worrying about Paige. Until the sun went down again...

He walked across the garage to the service door to the kitchen. After punching in the security code, he stepped into the kitchen with its rich cherry cabinets and white marble countertops. And he saw Paige's touch. She had decorated it as she'd done pretty much everything during their marriage—alone. Maybe that was why she hadn't wanted it in the divorce: it held too many memories for her. Or maybe she'd wanted him to have it more than she'd wanted to keep it. Maybe despite how little he'd shared with her, she'd known that the house had become something to him that he'd never known growing up. A home.

After his mom had died, he'd been shuffled from foster home to foster home, and to group homes when he'd gotten older. Because no one had been able to locate the father who'd taken off when his mom had first gotten sick, no one had been able or willing to adopt him for fear that his father would come back and take him away.

Unlike Paige's father, his had never come

back. Just as Paige had never come back to this house; it had to be that it held too many painful memories for her. While he'd told her about his past, he'd never really shared with her what it meant to him—that he'd become a cardiologist because of the helplessness he'd felt watching his mother slowly die of heart failure.

He opened the fridge to look for an ice pack for his ribs. But he didn't care about his own injuries. He cared about Paige. He should be with her, taking care of her.

But she wouldn't let him now…even though she had a stalker. Maybe after last night, she would finally admit she had one; that it wasn't all a mistake. But then there was so much Paige insisted on denying. Like her feelings for him.

They were still there; he saw them every time she looked at him, her gorgeous blue eyes soft with emotion. Every time she touched him, her affection flowed over him with sweet generosity. She might admit to having a stalker now, but he doubted she would admit to her feelings about him. What was the point, since they had both already agreed they had no future? They only had a past.

One he'd screwed up. A pain jabbed his chest,

but it wasn't from his ribs. He didn't need an ice pack right now. All he needed was a soft bed and as many hours of sleep as he could manage before someone paged him.

Actually, all he needed was Paige.

He headed up the back stairwell to his bedroom. The *master* bedroom, but it had always been more Paige's than his, with its periwinkle walls and lacy curtains and spread. He should have moved out when she had; he should have sold the house.

But he'd kept holding out hope that she would change her mind. That after she'd taken the time she'd needed alone, she would come home. But she'd never come back to this house. The last of his hope had evaporated when she'd had him served with divorce papers. But still he hadn't sold the house…even after he'd signed the papers, unwilling to fight with her then when they'd both been hurting so much.

He pushed open the door to his bedroom. With the wooden shades closed at the windows, it was dark, the darkness beckoning him to bed. After some sleep, he would talk to Paige whether she liked it or not. And this time he'd get through to her; she had to give up the club. And maybe, after he got through to her about that, he would attempt to talk to her about some other things, things they should have talked about four years ago.

He stepped into the master bath, off the bedroom, brushed his teeth, then headed toward the bed, dropping his clothes as he approached. He pulled back the blanket and crawled between the cool sheets. But when he shifted, warmth reached out to him, from the blankets and from the naked, curvy body next to his. "What the hell!"

"Don't you mean *who* the hell?" Paige murmured as she struggled to fully awaken.

"Damn it, Paige," he cursed her, "you shocked the hell out of me."

Out of herself, too. After she'd been released from the hospital, she had insisted Sebastian drop her here. She couldn't believe she'd actually come back to this house. She'd been reeling from the memories and emotions since she'd walked in the door, the one where Ben had carried her over the threshold when they'd moved in ten years ago. Having lived in a loft the first few years of their marriage, it had been their first real home.

Ever. Except for the foster homes in which Ben had lived, their single mothers had never been able to afford a house, or to provide them with security. Ben's because she'd been too sick and physically weak; Paige's because she'd just been too weak.

With as much as they'd had in common, it was no wonder that Paige had fallen for him. They should have been able to make their marriage work; they should have been able to have a lasting relationship.

She struggled again, not to awaken, but to bury the memories and the emotions. What they had now wasn't about the past or the future. It was the here and now, and that was all she would allow herself to think about.

"Are you all right?" he asked.

"Fine. It was just a scratch."

"A scratch doesn't require stitches."

"I'm fine," she insisted. "In fact, I think I'm better than you are." She couldn't see him in the darkened room, but there was something about his tone that revealed his tension.

"I'm…just shocked that you're here," he said.

"You're not used to women sneaking into your house to wait naked in your bed for you to come home?" she teased, willing to play any role—even the jealous ex-wife.

"The alarm usually stops them."

Her heartbeat accelerated as the emotions crept back in. "You didn't change the code." And she couldn't help but wonder why. For the same reason she'd used it as hers, probably because it was easy to remember.

"No," he said, his body taut next to hers, as if he didn't dare touch her. "I didn't."

She had to know. "Because you didn't think I'd come back or you didn't want to keep me out if I did?" she asked, holding her breath for his answer.

"Probably both."

"Don't worry," she assured him. "I'm not here to stay." She was brave enough now to visit, but she could never come home again even though he had asked her to move back in. To protect her. Only to protect her...

"Why are you here, Paige?" He kept to his side of the bed, something he'd never done when they were married. "Is this about playing another game? Who are you tonight?"

Someone who owed him an apology and, damn him, he was going to make her say it.

"I have something I need to tell you," she admitted.

Taking off her clothes and crawling into his bed had been insurance so that he would accept her apology, and so that things could go back to the uncomplicated fun and games they'd been having. Well, as uncomplicated as anything could ever be between the two of them.

"*You* want to talk?" he asked, his voice deepening with surprise.

She sucked in a breath and confessed, "I owe you an apology."

"Really?"

Damn him. He was going to force her to say all of it.

"You were right," she admitted with a grimace she hoped he couldn't see in the dark room, the only light spilling through the partially open bathroom door. "You had every reason to be worried about me, about my safety."

He expelled a weary-sounding sigh. "I'm sorry…that I was…right."

"Yeah, me, too. I just don't understand…I don't know why someone would come after me now. I'm not practicing law anymore."

"Why?" he asked again. "Why did you quit now?"

"When I hadn't when you asked me to?"

"I just wanted you to take it easy."

Would it have made a difference? Now she'd never know, and she would never forgive herself for taking the risk. "I didn't leave by choice," she admitted, too tired and scared to worry about her pride.

"Turrell fired you? After all those years you worked your ass off for him?"

She could have argued the point about her ass, as she still had plenty of it left. But she shrugged instead. "He probably thinks I had something to do with his wife finally deciding to divorce him."

"Did you?"

"I wouldn't have been a good friend if I hadn't." If only she'd been as good a wife…

"You can still practice law," Ben pointed out.

She shrugged again. "Maybe I finally took your advice. I thought owning the club would be easy."

"You couldn't have been more wrong," he remarked with a ragged sigh. "After all that's happened, do you see now that you need to stay away from Club Underground?"

Flashing back to the attack in the dark, she couldn't argue with him. She had to concede, "I hate being scared."

Ben rolled onto his side so that he faced her, his eyes aglow in the dark. "I want you to be scared, Paige."

She tensed with her own shock. "Why?"

"Then you'll be more aware and more careful," he explained, "and this stalker won't be able to hurt you. Again."

But Ben would. She shouldn't have come here. She should have left things between them as they were, with Ben thinking she wanted him to stay away from her. But then he touched her, sliding his hand over her bare shoulder, down her arm to her hip. Desire flooded her, heating her skin and hardening her nipples, and she remembered why she hadn't been able to stay away.

"I don't know what I'd do if something happened to you," he said, his voice raspy as emotion choked him. His fingers clenched her hip, pulling her closer.

Paige's heart contracted, and she fought for breath. "You don't know me," she said.

"God, isn't that the truth?" he murmured against her shoulder as he nibbled her skin.

She shivered. "No, I'm a stranger who's broken into your house."

Amusement lifted his lips, against her skin. "Are you looking for the safe under my pillow?"

She shook her head, sending her hair cascading around her shoulders, across his face. "No, you caught me, so I'm trying to convince you to let me go."

"Oh, Paige…"

"Shh," she said, pressing her finger against his lips. "You don't know me. I'm just a desperate thief, trying to change your mind about calling the cops on me."

"So—" he flopped on his back and linked his hands behind his head "—convince me."

Paige sat up and leaned over him, so that first her hair, then her nipples brushed his skin. His breath shuddered out, and the muscles in his arms flexed as he gripped the pillow beneath his head. She rubbed her breasts against his chest, where his heart beat as wildly as hers. Then she kissed him, making love to his mouth with her lips and her tongue. Soft, sipping kisses, then hot, slippery ones as their tongues mated.

Still he refused to touch her, keeping his hands behind his head. So she moved. Sliding her lips down his throat, then along his shoulder, nipping and laving the bitten areas with her tongue.

His chest rose and fell with harsh breaths as she continued her torture: kissing every inch of his chest, sliding her tongue over his hard, flat nipples. She moved lower, dipping her tongue into his navel, sliding her mouth over the rippling muscles of his stomach. Then she gave her attention to the part of him that begged for her touch, throbbing and pulsing. She licked and lapped at the hard, long length of his erection before closing her lips around his cock and taking him deep in her mouth.

His head thrashed on the pillows as groans tore from his throat. She teased him, bringing him to the brink again and again, until his control snapped.

His hands came out from beneath the pillow and tangled in her hair, first holding her against him, then pulling her away. He pushed her back on the bed. His mouth took hers, in a hot, possessive kiss before he pulled back, kissing his way across her cheek, down her neck and shoulder, until finally his lips closed over her nipples, one, then the other, pulling and sucking.

"Ben…"

"You don't know my name," he reminded her as he lifted one of her legs and slid his wet, throbbing cock inside her. He moved, driving in and out, while she rose up from the bed, lifting her hips to take him deeper, to keep him inside her.

An orgasm slammed into her as he did. She sobbed as the pleasure stole her mind and her control. She wrapped one leg around him, pulling him deeper, taking as much of him as she could hold.

Again and again, he pounded into her. And again and again, she came. Finally, his orgasm spilled from him and into her. He collapsed on top of her, into her arms, his breathing harsh and ragged in her ear, his chest slick and hot against her breasts.

"Oh, God…" She shuddered as little orgasms went off like firecrackers after the grand finale.

"You convinced me," he said, groaning, as he pulled from her and flopped onto his back again.

Paige struggled for first her breath, then her voice. "You're not going to call the cops on me and report the break-in?"

"You didn't break in," he reminded her. "You knew the code."

"God, Paige," he said as he turned toward her. "That was crazy."

It was. She needed to stay away from him. Instead, she got closer every time, pulling him deeper and deeper inside her, until he became a part of her. She had thought she'd been strong to come here; she would have been stronger had she stayed away.

"I should go," she said, trying to sit up, but her limp muscles protested.

And so did Ben, catching her around the shoulders and pulling her against his chest. He groaned, then murmured, "Not yet."

"I don't think you have enough energy for another round," she teased. When she snuggled closer, he groaned again, so she pulled back. Her eyes having adjusted to the darkness and not clouded with her passion for him, she finally noticed the redness around his ribs. "What happened to you?"

"I'm fine." He dismissed her concern.

She pressed on his chest, and his handsome face twisted with a grimace. "You're not fine."

"I don't believe you when you claim it, either," he said with a slight grin.

As usual, he was trying to get the focus off himself, but she was having none of it this time. "What happened to you?"

"It's not a big deal," he assured her. "I just had a little accident."

Like that voice inside her head, Sebastian's words resonated with her: *He would do anything to protect you...even risk his own life.*

"You got hurt trying to figure out who my stalker is," she surmised.

He laughed and shook his head. "I'm a surgeon—not a police officer. I'll leave the investigating to your detective friend. What did Kate say? You must have called her last night to report what happened in your office."

She nodded.

"So how is her investigation coming?"

"She already has a suspect," Paige admitted.

"She does?"

She smiled and kissed his chest. "You."

"Me?"

She moved her head against his shoulder, nodding. "But don't worry. You're *her* suspect, not mine."

"That's something, I guess." He blew out a ragged breath, his pride obviously stinging. "Okay, I guess I can understand why she'd think that."

"But I don't, Ben," she assured him, pressing a kiss against his skin.

His dark eyes flared with passion, and he rolled her onto her back. "Paige…" he murmured as his mouth dipped toward hers.

But before he could kiss her, the beeper rattled on the nightstand, vibrating. "Damn!" he said, reaching for the device. He uttered a curse as he glanced at the screen. "I have to leave…."

"That's okay," she said, despite her body's protest. Her nipples had hardened, her clit pulsing, wet and ready for his possession. Again.

"No, it's not," he said, his voice vibrating like the beeper had, but with frustration. "You're here."

"Yes." But she shouldn't have come. Not to the house. Not to him. Because he never stayed with her—he was never there for her like he was for his patients. And she hated herself for being jealous of them. And she hated him a little for making her feel like that.

His hands skimmed over her bare shoulders, over her breasts, his palms brushing across the hardened nipples. "And we need to talk about that."

"If you stayed," she said, sliding her hand over his hip, to the part of him that was reawakening, hard and throbbing, "we wouldn't be talking."

He chuckled. "Wait for me. Stay here." He didn't wait for her agreement, just jumped out of bed and grabbed his clothes from the floor.

"Ben…"

"Don't leave."

As she watched him walk away from her again, she realized that he had never really belonged to her despite those vows they had taken.

She was in less danger from her stalker than she was from Ben. If she fell for him again, as deeply as she had before, there wouldn't be enough stitches to heal her wounds. Or her broken heart.

Chapter 11

Ringing echoed in Ben's ear until, finally, the answering machine picked up his call home. Not Paige. Had she left already?

God, if it had been any other patient needing him…

Hell, he still would have left. He'd taken an oath, but despite that, this patient was special. As her lashes fluttered open, he shut his cell. "Hey, there, sweetheart, how are you feeling?"

Weak. Even if he didn't know how thready her pulse and how low her oxygen levels, he would have recognized the weakness in the way the little girl could barely lift her lids or the corners of her usually smiling mouth.

Her blue eyes brightened as she recognized him, and she forced a smile and murmured, "G-g-good…"

"Liar," he gently accused her as he chucked her chin. His heart ached as he realized how fragile the child was. With her delicate build, she appeared younger than her nine-and-a-half years. But with all the surgeries she'd had to repair the birth defects to her heart, Adelaide Plumb had been through much more than people many years older than she was. "Where's your mother?"

"W-work…" But the child couldn't hold his gaze as she answered him, and he suspected she was lying again. Her single mother was rarely around, often not showing up until after visiting hours were over. Because of work or something else?

Ben suspected something else, but then, because of the secrets he'd learned and the way he'd grown up, he trusted no one.

"I'll catch up with your mother tonight," he said. "You need your rest, so you can recover from this last surgery." The one in which he'd repaired the hole in her heart. He resisted the urge, barely, to lean over and kiss her forehead as her eyes drifted closed again.

With her blond curls and pale skin, she reminded him of Paige. After leaving her room, he took the elevator down to the office level and unlocked the door that opened directly into his office, bypassing the reception area.

Groaning at the ache in his ribs, he dropped into the chair behind his desk and clicked the redial button on his cell. The phone rang and rang before the machine answered again.

"Paige, if you're there, pick up," he said, then grimaced as he realized he was ordering her, just as he had ordered her to stay. Paige never responded well to being told what to do or not to do.

She had probably already ignored his order for her to stay away from the club, too. But he needed to convince her that for her own safety, she could have nothing to do with Club Underground. At least with the sun shining brightly, streaking through the blinds at the office windows, he wasn't too worried about her being out alone. But he hoped like hell she was lying in that bed, waiting for him and listening to his voice on the machine.

"Paige…" God, he hated that he'd had to leave. His body hated him, too, tense with frustration despite what they'd done once. Once was never enough with Paige.

"If you're there, I'm sorry I had to leave," he apologized. "We have to talk."

Not just make love. If he'd stayed, he wouldn't have let her distract him again. Not after they'd made love one more time. "We *really* need to talk."

"I was thinking the same thing, Dr. Davison," said a dark-haired woman as she rapped her knuckles against the open door of the private entrance. He could have sworn he'd locked it behind himself.

Had she picked it like she'd tried to pick the lock of the door to the secret room in Club Underground? From the monitor screen, he recognized her dark hair and suit. She was the woman who'd been with Paige that night. But even if he hadn't recognized her, he would have realized who she was from the cynicism in her hard stare.

"Detective," he greeted her as he clicked shut his cell phone.

"Detective Wever," she clarified, holding her badge out for his inspection.

He took her hand, the one without the badge, and shook it. She had a firm grip, definitely a no-nonsense woman. "Detective Wever, it's nice to meet you."

"Sorry to interrupt your call," she said, without a trace of apology. "I couldn't help but notice that you seem a bit desperate to talk to your ex-wife."

"Paige warned me that I'm your number one suspect," Ben said as he settled deeper into his chair. "I appreciate that you're doing your job, but I don't want you wasting your time."

Kate tilted her head as if assessing him. "I don't waste *my* time."

Just his? A muscle twitched in his cheek, but he refused to let her rankle him. "That's good. Then you'll keep Paige safe."

She continued to study him, her blue eyes narrowed. "I intend to, by finding her stalker. I won't stop…until I stop *him*…from hurting Paige again."

"That's good." Except that now Ben had someone else to worry about because the relentless detective would undoubtedly uncover the secret that would get her killed.

"You don't sound that convinced," Kate observed. The woman was shrewd.

"I'm concerned," he assured her. "I'm worried about my wife."

"Your *ex*-wife," Kate reminded him.

"Right," he agreed, although he wondered if he would ever be able to think of Paige that way. God knew, for his sanity, he had to learn. He had to adjust to their being divorced.

"Don't you think of her as an ex?" the detective persisted, as if she'd read his mind. "Or do you still think of her as *yours?*"

He laughed. "Mine? I never thought of Paige as mine. You're her friend. You should know that Paige belongs only to herself. No one owns her."

The detective's blue eyes widened, as if she were impressed. "You've certainly evolved, Doctor."

"What?" He had no clue what she was talking about.

"Some men struggle with the issue of ownership."

She had to be talking about men she'd met while investigating cases of stalking or domestic abuse. Nothing personal. He couldn't imagine any man ever thinking he owned *her.*

"I own my car and my house. Nothing else, Detective," he said. Hell, he couldn't even call *his* life his own because of the damn secret society.

"Any other women in your life who might take exception to Paige still being part of it?" the detective asked, pen poised above her little spiral pad.

He ran a hand through his hair, wondering who was asking this question, the detective or the friend. "No."

"You hesitated, Doctor."

"Ben," he reminded her, then sighed wearily. He'd never gotten that sleep he'd wanted because he'd wanted something else more. "I hesitated because my complete answer won't reassure you about my intentions regarding Paige."

"Why not?"

He sighed, hating to make this admission more because of his pride than how it made him look as a suspect. "I haven't been with another woman since the divorce."

"Why, Ben?" she asked.

He didn't have to answer her question, because he knew he was talking to the friend now, not the detective. But he felt compelled to admit, "I would have felt like I was cheating on my wife."

Her blue eyes warming, she said, "That answer doesn't raise my suspicions, Ben."

"We're divorced. Being faithful to my ex-wife doesn't make me sound crazy?" Now he wanted the reassurance. He didn't have friends like Paige had. He only had Sebastian, whom Ben resented more than he trusted. And he couldn't risk anyone else finding out the secret he had to keep.

She smiled. "Nope, you sound like a man in love."

His heart clenched. Ironic that he could fix everyone else's heart but his own. Only Paige could fix his. "So does that take me off the suspect list or leave me at the top?"

Even though her smile didn't slip, she shook her head. "Stalkers are usually in love with their victims."

He couldn't deny that he was in love with Paige. But he knew that whoever threatened her life had no love for her—only hate.

As the door creaked open to total darkness, Paige sucked in a startled breath. She should have been used to Sebastian closing the blinds to block out all sunlight, so that he could sleep during the day and spend his nights wide awake. But it was so dark that she tripped over something strewn across the hardwood floor. She flipped on the light switch, then gasped. Everything had been overturned—every piece of furniture, every book from the shelves. Only shattered fragments remained of porcelain trinkets and vases.

"Sebastian!"

He stumbled out of his room; it wasn't legally a bedroom, as it had no windows. She had intended to use it as a den, but then Sebastian had needed a place to stay, claiming he'd lost the lease on his loft. She suspected that he'd actually been worried about her being alone after she'd divorced Ben. He hadn't had reason for his concern. *Then.*

"What the hell…?" he murmured, rubbing at his eyes.

"Are you okay?" she asked anxiously.

He blinked away the last of his sleep and met her gaze. "Yeah, yeah…"

"What happened here?"

He expelled a ragged breath. "Eh, would you believe a wild party?"

"No." Maybe when he'd first showed up at her door nearly ten years ago, but while it wasn't apparent that he'd physically aged—he took after their father in that respect, he had grown maturity-wise. He had not taken after their father in that respect. Or so she'd thought. "What happened?"

He shrugged. "I don't know. It was like this when I got back from dropping you off at Ben's. Did Ben bring you back here?"

She shook her head. "I called a cab."

Anger flashed in his blue eyes. "Ben wouldn't drive you home?"

"He had to leave."

Sebastian nodded with understanding; he'd always been more accepting of the demands on Ben's time than she had ever been. "So he called you a cab?"

"Actually, he asked me to stay until he got back," she admitted. Stepping over all her personal property strewn around the living room, she shuddered and wished now that she had.

Sebastian shook his head. "But instead of staying, you called a cab?"

"I...I thought it was hypocritical of him," she

explained, "to want me to stay when he never does."

"Paige—"

"I don't want to talk about Ben. I want to talk about what happened here." She glanced back to the door. "Were we broken into?"

He shrugged. "I don't know. I stopped back last night before going to the club. I might have forgotten to put the alarm back on."

"And you forgot to lock the door?"

He pushed his hands through his hair. "I don't know. I wasn't thinking…."

She couldn't be a hypocrite herself and berate him for his lapse when she'd just had one of her own. She never should have gone back to that house, back to Ben. But, remembering what they'd done in their old bed, her body tightened with frustration over their not doing it again and proved her a liar. She should have waited for him to come back from the hospital and finish what else they'd started.

But she hadn't been able to stay alone in that house, not any longer, not without the memories strangling her. How could he continue to live there? Maybe he didn't remember as much as she did; maybe he didn't care as much.

"You should call Ben," Sebastian said.

"W-why?"

"He'll want to know that you got home safely," he said then sighed again. "And he'll want to know about this…"

She shook her head. "There's nothing Ben can do here. I need to call the police instead."

"Call Ben, too," Sebastian urged.

"He was wrong," she pointed out. "He thinks I'm only in danger at the club."

He hadn't been alone in that belief, though. She had thought so, too. But as she stared at the destruction of her living room—at the violation of her privacy—she lifted trembling fingertips to the bandage on her throat. And she realized that it didn't matter where she was—at Club Underground or home—she was in danger.

Chapter 12

Sebastian winced as Ben pulled the needle through his skin, pulling closed the gaping wound over his ribs. A curse slipped out of his clenched teeth.

"Hold still," Ben admonished him. "You're going to be damn lucky if this doesn't get infected."

He'd gotten damn lucky that Paige hadn't noticed the blood seeping through his makeshift bandage or she would have insisted he go to the hospital. And the bright sunlight would have done him more damage than the sharp point of the wooden stake had.

Another sharp point of the needle jabbed through his skin again. "Son of a bitch…"

"Hey, you've never met my mother," Ben said with a short chuckle but no humor.

Because Sebastian had checked out the man with whom his daughter had fallen in love, he knew all about Ben's past. Dr. Davison had only made the comment to distract Sebastian from the pain he was never quite able to numb him from feeling. "I know what you're doing and that your mother is dead."

Ben sighed. "My first failure…"

"You were ten when she died," Sebastian said, frustrated with how much responsibility Ben took on himself. But then some people had to make up for men like him, who'd never take on their own responsibilities. "You grew up in foster homes after that. Then group homes when you got older."

Although his hands remained steady as he worked, Ben lifted his shoulders in a slight shrug. "It wasn't that bad."

It hadn't been that good, either, Sebastian suspected, but yet Ben had grown up strong, smart and ambitious. He would have been a good husband and father…if not for Sebastian screwing that all up for him…and for Paige.

Trouble was the last thing he'd intended to cause his daughter when he sought her out. He'd only wanted to be part of her life. And to protect her. He grimaced, but it had nothing to do with the needle pulling his skin. "Seems like we're making a habit of this…."

"Me sewing you up?" Ben asked, then nodded. "Yeah, it's a bad habit. So you didn't get a look at who was waiting in Paige's condo?"

"No." Rage throbbed along with the pain of Sebastian's cuts and bruises. "I got jumped in the dark." By someone brandishing a damn wooden stake. "Like Paige, I had no idea if it was a man or woman or…"

"Beast?"

The Underground didn't consist of just the secret vampire society; other creatures existed there and had sought Ben's medical help in the past.

Thinking of some of the werewolves and shape-shifters Sebastian had met during his many, many years living in the Underground, he shuddered in revulsion. "I'm just glad I dropped Paige at your house before coming home."

"Because they were really after *her.*"

Dread tied Sebastian's stomach into knots. "It looks that way." He'd hoped it was him—that the flowers and the damage to the car had all been warnings to him. But after she'd been attacked in her office, it appeared that Paige was really the one in danger.

"How the hell are we going to keep her safe?" Ben asked. "She's too stubborn to listen to reason. She won't stop coming around here." With the needle still in his hand, he gestured toward the locked door that opened onto the back hallway of the club.

"No, she won't," Sebastian agreed. "The only way we can keep her safe is to stick close to her."

A muscle twitched along Ben's tightly clenched jaw. "I can't…"

"She had me drop her off at your place last night," Sebastian reminded his friend. "She may say she wants you to stay away from her, but she doesn't really want that."

"She's not the reason I can't stick close to her," Ben said.

"Then I don't understand…." Because he knew the man still loved Paige—that he had never stopped.

"I can't because of you," the doctor explained. "You and *them*. I wasn't there for her the last time she needed me. Because I have to come every time one of you—one of them—calls."

"I'm sorry." No matter how many times he said it…his guilt never lessened. Because the damn words made no difference; they couldn't change what had happened, they couldn't bring back everything that Ben had lost.

All Sebastian could do was try to make sure that Ben lost nothing more—not Paige's life or his own.

When they'd been married, she'd invited Ben to Happy Hour several times, but he had never been able to make the time to meet her friends. Then. What the hell was he doing here now?

She had been too busy, working back in the office, to realize that her friends had arrived and had taken the table in the quiet corner. But Ben was there. And it didn't look quiet, as everyone had their heads thrown back, laughing.

At what? Her?

Had to be over her because Ben had never told anything but lame jokes. How could such a brilliant man have such a limited sense of humor? Well, he had to have one fault. Not that her friends, the traitorous bitches who fawned over him, found any fault with him. Not even Kate, who Paige had thought considered him *public* enemy number one. Well, maybe not public enemy, just Paige's enemy. And what about Lizzy, whose hand lay on Ben's arm? Where had Paige's divorce lawyer's loyalty gone?

She could understand Renae laughing, since Ben was her superior at the hospital. Dr. Grabill might want to make a good impression. But the other women…Paige had thought better of them. They had never gone all giggly and giddy over a man before, any man. That was why they were Paige's friends.

She walked straight over to that usually quiet booth. When she joined them, the laughter died down as everyone turned to her.

"Paige, join us," Ben, the interloper, invited. "Unless you're tending bar now?"

She shook her head and held up her water bottle. "No, just grabbing a drink."

"You look good on that side of the bar," he remarked. His dark eyes flared with desire as he shared the memory with her, of the two of them making love on the hard, polished surface.

Her face heated, her nipples hardening beneath the thin silk of the red blouse she wore with a black velvet skirt and knee-high leather boots.

"Ben, what are you doing here?" she asked.

"I've been getting to know your friends," he said, flashing his wide grin at the women sitting around him.

Paige was more concerned with *their* getting to know *him*. But the buzz of the beeper in his shirt pocket allayed her fears. "You have to go," she said. "I'm sorry."

He winked at her, obviously aware that she wasn't. "Yes, I have to go."

His new fan club uttered protests at his leaving. "Oh, you haven't been here very long."

Paige inwardly grimaced at their remarks even while she held on to her smile. "Maybe he can come back another time," she suggested.

Like when hell froze over.

"Please stick close to her, Kate," he implored the brunette, dropping his voice so only the detective, who sat on the end of the booth near him, and Paige could hear. "She refuses to be careful."

She couldn't argue with him, because if she was being careful, she would avoid him at all costs.

When Ben stood up, his body brushed hers, and he whispered in her ear, "I'll see you later."

She lifted a brow, challenging his claim.

"Naked," he promised, then asked, "In my bed or yours?"

Her breath caught in her lungs. Helpless to resist her attraction to him, she answered him in a voice husky with desire. "Mine."

"Staking claim?" Campbell asked, as all the women watched Ben walk away. But they weren't the only ones watching him. Everyone in the club followed him with their eyes—his broad shoulders, his long strides—the man had more than sex appeal. He was magnetic; no wonder Paige couldn't stay away from him.

She blinked. "What?"

"You called him mine."

She shook her head, then settled into the booth next to Elizabeth. "Not anymore. Lizzy helped me take care of that four years ago."

"He doesn't hold it against me," Lizzy said, "thank goodness."

"I can't believe you divorced Dr. Davison," Renae said, shaking her head in disbelief.

"Couples have many reasons for getting divorced," admitted the divorce lawyer.

Campbell nodded. "A lot more reasons to get divorced than to get married. Especially when it's so hard to figure out who it's safe to trust."

Kate's lips lifted into a small smile. "I had to tell them what was going on with you, Paige, so that I could find out if they'd noticed anything suspicious."

The other women started peppering her with questions about her investigation. Paige was almost relieved to discuss the scary incidents that had happened. She would much rather talk about her stalker than Ben.

"You really impressed my friends tonight," Paige said as she collapsed onto Ben's chest, slick with perspiration, boneless with satisfaction. Just as he'd promised, he'd been waiting in her bed, naked, when she'd come home from the club. And she'd quickly joined him.

"What about you?" he asked between ragged breaths, his chest pushing against her breasts as it rose and fell.

She pressed a kiss to his shoulder. "I think you know how much you impress me."

He rubbed his hand over her naked back, kneading her shoulders. "And if you impressed me any more, Paige, I'd be dead."

"Heart surgeon dies from heart attack," she mused, repeating his remarks from the other day, but, of course, she left off the "brilliant" part. "Talk about irony."

"Yes," he agreed, "let's talk about irony, like two divorced people who can't get enough of each other."

Enough. That was what she needed to call this.

"We are divorced," she said, hoping that if she kept repeating it, she might remember. "So I'd understand if you didn't want to spend so much time with me."

His hands stilled on her back, then moved up and around to cup her face. "Paige?"

"What I—I mean," she stammered, and she never stammered, "if you've been seeing someone else…"

"When?" He lowered his brows, as if trying to figure out when he would have managed that. "You know how my job is. It's amazing I find as much time to be with you as I do."

"That's what I mean," she said, "that I shouldn't be taking up all your free time."

He sighed, both wearily and wistfully. "I wished I'd spent more time with you when we were married."

Then they might still be married? She hoped he didn't believe that...even if he might be right.

"We both have regrets," Paige admitted, closing her eyes as all hers washed over her again.

"Let's talk about those," he urged.

She shook her head, pulling it free from his hands. "No. That's the past. There's no sense in rehashing all that."

He obviously didn't agree, as he opened his mouth to argue, "Paige—"

She laid her fingers across his lips. "I want to talk about *now,* about how it's not fair that you're spending all your time with me." When he'd probably be much happier with someone, with anyone, else. "Don't feel that you have to—"

"Paige, I want to."

"Because you think I'm in danger." She pressed a kiss to his jaw, which was so tense a muscle twitched in his cheek. "It's sweet that you want to protect me, but it's not fair to you that I'm taking all your free time."

"Even without the stalker, I'd want to spend

all my free time with you, Paige." He tipped up her chin and pressed his kiss to her lips.

Moved by his words, she felt her heart shudder. Against his mouth, she murmured, "Oh, Ben…"

Her nipples hardened, brushing against the soft hair on his chest as she breathed deep through her nose, her mouth molded to his. His tongue slipped through her lips, sliding over hers, teasing, tasting.

She moaned and shifted, brushing just the tips of her breasts against his chest, tormenting them both. She parted her legs, so that her heat rubbed against his erection.

"I can't believe you want me again," she murmured as she slid her lips from his, over his jaw, down his throat.

"Always." He worked his hands, his clever, healing hands, between their bodies.

He pushed her until she sat up, straddling him. Then his palms cupped her breasts, massaging them while his thumbs flicked back and forth across her sensitive nipples. He rose up, just enough, that he could close his mouth over one of the peaks, tugging with his lips and teeth until she convulsed and shuddered, an orgasm spilling from her.

Beneath her, his cock became hot and hard. She eased up and closed her hand over him. She rubbed the glistening tip of his erection against her clit. She bit her lip, trying to hold in a moan, as another orgasm ripped through her. "Ben…"

"Let me in, Paige," he beseeched her, his cock throbbing in her hand.

She slid the length of him inside her. Her muscles closed around him, holding him tight. Then she rose up, riding him up and down.

His hands closed over her hips, lifting and slamming her back down, while his mouth continued to feast on her breasts.

She bit her lip again, but she couldn't hold in the moan, "Ben…"

"Say my name," he ordered her.

"Ben…"

His hand moved between them, his fingers stroking over her clit. Her toes curled as her inner muscles convulsed, and an intense orgasm tore through her. She reached behind her butt, sliding her hand up his inner thigh, touching him.

He groaned and shouted her name as he came. He stiffened and shuddered, then collapsed back on the bed.

Paige melted onto his heaving chest.

"Paige," he murmured sleepily, his lips lifted in a small, satisfied smile.

She pushed her hair out of her face, lifting her head to meet his gaze. But his eyes were closed, his chest moving more easily now as his breathing relaxed. And he slept.

In her bed.

It wasn't fair. She needed to tell him that they had no future, only a past that bound them so tightly they weren't quite able to walk away.

But Paige knew telling him to leave now would be pointless. Until the stalker was caught, he was determined to stick close to her, to protect her. But who would protect her from him…from getting her heart broken once the stalker was caught and he left again?

Chapter 13

His pulse racing, Ben pulled back the curtain in the Emergency Room. Because he had braced himself for the worst, he drew a sigh of relief at finding Paige sitting atop the gurney.

"What happened?" he asked, unable to completely relax even though she was conscious. "Why are you here?"

She gestured toward her throat.

"Oh, God, you were attacked again?" But she was alive—did that mean that she would always be alive? That she'd been turned?

Yet he doubted she'd be conscious, then. The line between being turned into an undead and being dead was a very fine line—one few mortals had successfully crossed. Or else the society would not have remained as secret as it had for all these centuries.

"No." Paige shook her head. "Renae took out the stitches." She furrowed her brow in confusion at his over-reaction. "I'm fine."

His heart slowed. "I heard you were here, and I…"

"…expected the worst?" she asked.

"That's been the case lately."

Hurt flashed in her blue eyes. "Has it?"

"Except for us," he said. With as close as they'd been lately, he'd begun to believe that they might be able to try again—and make their relationship work.

But as he noted the faint scar on her neck, he reminded himself that wasn't possible. He knew something she could never learn. And with the secret between them, they could have nothing else.

"Us?" she asked, the confusion remaining on her face and in the depths of those bright blue eyes. "We're not an us anymore. If we ever were…"

"We were," he insisted. "We were happy."

"We were busy," she said. "You with your medicine. Me with my law practice. I've changed." She uttered an ironic chuckle. "Not by choice."

"You could still practice law," he pointed out. She would be a helluva lot safer if she did. "Firms would fight over you. Or you could open your own practice."

"I could," she agreed.

"You can't really want to continue running the club," he persisted, "not after everything that's happened there."

She smiled. "I'm not a quitter."

"You're not?" he challenged, as resentment overtook his earlier concern for her. "You're the one who filed for divorce."

Her smile slid away, leaving only pain and her own resentment. "You'd quit us long before I filed."

"Paige…"

"And the only reason you keep coming back is because you're worried about me," she accused him.

He stepped closer, parting her thighs to stand between her legs. Leaning over her, his lips brushing her earlobe, he murmured, "We both know that's not the only reason I can't stay away from you…."

She shivered. "Ben…"

He slid his mouth from her ear, across her cheek to her lips. In her kiss, he tasted her anger and passion. And the resentment she harbored yet for his not being there when she'd needed him most.

"Oops," a feminine voice exclaimed.

Paige pushed at his chest, shoving him back. "Renae—"

"I'm sorry," the young trauma surgeon said, her face pink with embarrassment. "I didn't mean to interrupt. I'll come back."

"No!" Paige wriggled down from the bed. "You took out the stitches. I can leave now, right?"

Dr. Grabill glanced to Ben, as if seeking his approval. Probably because he had earned the respect of his fellow physicians.

He hadn't earned his ex-wife's, though, as she ignored him and said, "I have to get back to the club."

"It's not open yet," Ben pointed out, fully aware that she was now using the club as an excuse to get away from him. He wished her luck, because distance had never gained him any perspective. He had yet to figure out a way to keep his secret *and* Paige.

She lifted her wrist and glanced at her watch. "But there are deliveries scheduled soon. I need to be there to accept them."

"Sebastian is there." The vampire was always there. "He'll sign for them. He doesn't need you…like I need you."

Renae cleared her throat. "I…I'll leave you two alone, then."

"No!" Panic shone brightly in Paige's eyes. She didn't want to be alone with him; she didn't trust him with her heart anymore.

He didn't blame her.

"I'm on duty," Ben said. "I have to stay here in the hospital. But there's someone here that I want you to meet."

"You're on duty," Paige said. "We'll have to do this another time."

"I'll answer your pages," Renae offered. Unrepentant, she smiled when Paige glared at her and held out her hand for his beeper.

Ben reached for it, holding it tight in his palm for a moment before passing it over. It was daylight; no one from the Underground would need him.

God, if only it was daylight all the time.

His hand empty, he closed it around Paige's and tugged her along with him. She sputtered and protested but followed him into the elevator. A slow day at the hospital found them alone in the small car.

So Ben took advantage of the privacy and her. Pulling her into his arms, he covered her mouth with his.

A creak out in the hall drew Sebastian's attention from the paperwork strewn across his desk—Paige's desk since she'd claimed it as hers. He had to get her to back away from the club. Completely.

"Paige?" he called out.

She'd insisted on coming in early to accept delivery of this week's shipments. He'd tried to argue her out of it—as she had no idea what was included in the club's supplies. And he wanted to keep it that way—with her entirely in the dark. She had to literally be in the dark out in the hall as the bulbs must have burned out of the wall sconces.

"Paige, I'm in the office," he called out again, hoping she wasn't trying to get into the secret room again. Another reason he needed to keep her away from the club. She was entirely too curious about it. But with good reason.

She had never asked him many questions; she had easily accepted his claim that he was her brother. She'd accepted him as family. He didn't deserve her loyalty or her love.

If she only knew the truth about him.

And yet another reason he needed to keep her away from the club—his fear that she might discover not just the society's secrets, but his as well.

"I thought you were going to be at the hospital," he said, as he rose from behind the desk. "That sexy doctor friend of yours has to take out your stitches."

Usually any reference to her friends got a rise out of Paige, but there was no disapproving remark forthcoming. Only another clang—of metal against metal as the door to the secret room opened. His blood slowed in his veins with dread and foreboding. It wasn't Paige in the hall.

While it was dark in the club, it was daylight outside—the time that members of the secret society were forced to go *literally* underground. If not for the deliveries today, he would have been back at the condo—sleeping in his windowless room. Now he was wide awake, his heart beating hard as he stepped into the dark hall.

The metal creaked again, drawing his attention to the end of the hall and the door that stood ajar. A faint light filtered between the steel and the jamb.

"Ben?" The surgeon was probably stocking his makeshift O.R. with supplies. It had to be Ben.

But no one responded.

"Ingrid?" He shuddered at the thought of being alone with the pit viper. To think he'd once hit on her...but that was before he'd noticed her crazy eyes.

Of course he hadn't earned his womanizing reputation by being discriminating. He pressed his hand against his chest. Even through two layers of cotton, he could feel the ridge of the old scar from when Ben had saved his eternal life—after one of his psycho exes had tried to take it.

Hell, he'd rather think it was rats than Ingrid in the secret room. But the rats wouldn't have been able to open the door.

He sucked in a deep breath and pushed open the door—and his blood stopped flowing entirely. "Oh, God, it's *you*...."

The blond-haired woman turned away from where she stood over Ben's table. Her hand was bleeding from a wound caused by the scalpel she grasped. She stared at him—her eyes far more full of madness than Ingrid's had ever been.

"What are you doing here?" he asked. She had been gone so long, so deep in hiding, that he'd almost convinced himself she would never come back.

"I killed you once," she mused as she watched her own blood fall—one drop at a time onto the stainless steel table. "I killed you but you're still here."

"You don't want to do this," he said as he forced his patented charming smile.

"Because of him...that doctor..." The hatred shone brighter, her bitterness shrill as she demanded, "*Call* that doctor!"

Sebastian shook his head. "This isn't about him...or about my sister. You're the one who attacked her."

"Your sister?" She laughed. "She's your *daughter*."

"You know?"

"It's about as secret as the society."

"Paige has nothing to do with the society. She doesn't know about it. She doesn't know that I'm her father." He glanced around the room, looking for a weapon—some way to overpower her so that she wouldn't try to hurt him again or herself.

After she'd shoved the stake in his chest the last time, she'd lifted one to her own. He'd had just enough strength left to stop her then.

"She's not the only one."

His attention snapped back to her. "What do you mean?"

"You've lived up to your *virile* reputation, Sebastian."

"You're saying that you had my baby?" He swallowed hard. "But we haven't been together for years."

"She's nine."

He gasped his surprise. She'd been pregnant then—when they'd fought over that stake….

"She's so beautiful. And sick. So very sick, and *your doctor* can't fix her. He tries." Bitterness and disdain twisted her mouth into a grotesque scowl. "But he can't."

"Ben can," Sebastian promised. "He'll save her."

She shook her head. "No, he can't."

"Isn't that why you want him to come here?" he asked, trying to reason with her. But the last time he'd tried, he'd wound up with a stake in his heart. "You want him to help you and her?"

She shook her head again. "No."

"Then why are you here?" he asked to buy himself some time. He had no doubt as to her intentions.

She lifted her other hand, the one that wasn't bleeding. And in it she held a wooden stake, the point honed sharp. "I'm here to kill you. And this time I'm going to make damn sure he doesn't bring you back."

Passion flooded Paige, heating her blood. Her skin burned everywhere that Ben touched her. And he touched her everywhere, running his hands down her back to her hips. He pulled her tight against him, where his erection throbbed behind his fly.

A bell dinged, forewarning the opening doors. And Ben's withdrawal. Breathing hard, he pulled back but kept his fingers entwined with hers. She followed him, eagerly now, down another hall. Instead of leading her to his private office, though, he led her to a room…and a fragile patient sitting up in her bed as she colored a piece of paper on her bedside table.

"Hey, sweetheart," Ben murmured as he dropped Paige's hand and settled on the bed next to the child.

"Hey, Doc," the little girl said, a smile brightening her face and blue eyes as she gazed up at him. "I'm drawing you a picture."

Paige's heart ached with regret and loss. She struggled to process the image before her—the child who could have been theirs…had she not lost their baby and the chance to give her husband any more children.

"I brought a friend to meet you," Ben said, holding out his hand for Paige to join them. "This is Addi."

Addi giggled. "Only Dr. D. calls me Addi. My name is Adelaide."

Paige's legs trembled with the urge to flee the room, but she forced herself to walk toward the bed. "Hello, Adelaide."

"This is Paige," Ben said, introducing them. "She's very special to me…like you are."

The child met her gaze, and despite her youth, the wisdom of an old soul shone from the depths of her eyes. "You can call me Addi, too," she offered. Then she held out the picture she'd been working on of a house with two adults and one little blond-haired girl standing beside a dog.

"Very nice," Paige praised her. "Is that your family?"

Addi shook her head. "I don't have a family."

Paige's stomach pitched in reaction. She had no family, either…not since she'd lost her baby.

"You have a mom," Ben reminded the child. "She works really hard—that's why she can't be here with you."

Like he wasn't there for Paige when she'd needed him—because he'd been working.

"I know," the child murmured, lowering her gaze to her picture—her eyes filled with longing for what she'd wanted but believed she would never have.

"Oh, honey…" Paige sighed, recognizing a kindred wounded spirit. She joined Ben on the bed and pushed her fingers through the child's blond curls. "It's okay that you don't understand, that you want your mom here with you instead of at work."

"That doesn't make me selfish?" Addi asked.

Paige shook her head. "No, it just means you love her a lot and want her with you."

Addi stared up at her, confusion clouding her eyes along with fatigue. "I don't know…."

Paige's arms ached with the need to close around the child and comfort her. But Ben tugged her up.

"You need to rest, Addi," he told the little girl.

Her thick lashes fluttered over her closing eyes. But she fought to keep her lids open and her gaze fixed on Paige. "You'll come see me again?"

Paige nodded. It might kill her…to face everything she'd once longed for and lost, but she would. "I will. I'll come back."

A smile curved Addi's lips as her eyes closed and she slipped into a deep slumber.

"What's wrong with her?" Paige asked, turning to Ben the minute he led her back into the hall.

"She had some birth defects to her heart. It's been a long road for her, but I think she'll be fine now."

"You think?"

"There are no guarantees."

"No, there aren't," she agreed as she followed him into the elevator again. They weren't alone, but even if they had been, she doubted they would have fallen into each other's arms.

But he caught her hand and pulled her off onto the floor of professional offices. "I have to go to the club," she reminded him.

"Not until we talk." He tugged her along to his office, unlocking the door that bypassed the reception and opened directly into his private suite of rooms. An office and a bathroom.

She wanted to use the bathroom—to splash cool water on her face. To brace herself for what she knew and dreaded was about to come.

They were going to have that talk…the one she'd put off for four years. Paige and Ben needed to make a clean break, and that wouldn't happen until they did what she dreaded most. Until they talked about what had happened.

What did the shrinks call it? Closure. Because she'd walked away the way she had, they'd never gotten closure to their relationship.

"Why'd you take me to meet Addi?" she asked.

"You know why."

She nodded. "How do you work on her… without thinking of…"

"Of the child we lost?" he asked. "I can't. I think of her every time I see Addi."

Chapter 14

"I try not to think of her at all," Paige admitted. "It hurts too much." She pressed a hand to her chest now, to her aching heart, and she fought to catch her breath.

"It's been four years, Paige. We need to talk about her, about what happened."

"What's to talk about?" she asked. "We both know what happened and why. It was my fault."

"No!"

She nodded as tears stung her eyes and hysteria bubbled out of her, "It was. I…I didn't slow down like you wanted me to. I kept working long hours at the firm and doing the pro bono work for the public defender's office. That's why I developed preeclampsia…how… how I nearly died. It's how I killed our *baby.*"

Strong hands closed around her shoulders and shook her gently. "Paige, stop it, it wasn't your fault." His arms closed around her, pulling her tight against him. "I had no idea that you blamed yourself."

She swallowed hard, choking on emotion. "You *blamed* me, too. That's why you pulled away from me. Why you spent even less time with me than you had."

"No!" he hotly denied. Too hotly. "I *never* blamed you." He held her more tightly. "And I wasn't the one who pulled away, Paige. You were the one who filed for divorce."

Oh, God, the pain ripped through her as she wrestled with the memories. That was why she had avoided this talk for so long. "And you didn't fight me," she reminded him, "because you blamed me."

He sucked in a deep breath. "I don't blame you, Paige."

"Well, that makes one of us."

His voice full of wonder, he asked, "You've been blaming yourself this whole time?"

She nodded, biting her lip to hold in the sobs burning her throat. But she couldn't fight back the tears anymore, and they spilled from her eyes.

"God, Paige." He pulled back and pushed a hand through her hair, sweeping it back from her damp face. "I thought you blamed *me.*"

Confused, she blinked away the tears to stare up at him. "Why would I blame *you?*"

"Because I was never there for you when you needed me," he said, his voice hoarse with self-disgust. "I'm a doctor. I should have recognized the symptoms."

"It came on suddenly," she reminded him. "The blood pressure rising. The swelling. The headaches."

"But if I'd been with you, I would have realized what was about to happen. The placenta abruption…the hemorrhaging…" He shuddered. "I didn't just lose a child. I nearly lost you, too!"

"That wasn't *your* fault," she insisted. She slid her arms around his lean waist and hugged him close, absorbing his guilt through the fierce beat of his heart against hers. "I was working too hard. I wasn't taking care of myself or our baby."

"You nearly died," Ben said, his voice cracking with emotion. "I never would have forgiven myself. I'm there for my patients—no matter who—but I wasn't there for my wife or my baby. I wouldn't blame you if you hated me. I thought you did. That's why I didn't fight the divorce."

"I don't hate you, Ben." If only she could. Her life would be much simpler. But nothing had ever been simple about her feelings for this man.

"You should," he said. "I failed you."

And for a man like him, a man who was almost superhuman with his life-saving abilities, any failure hit him hard.

"You're only human," she reminded him, because sometimes she needed to remind herself. "You couldn't be everywhere at once."

"I should have been with you." He cupped her face in his palms and tilted it up as he leaned down. His lips brushed across her eyes, which must have been swollen from her tears. "I should have been there for you before…"

"I lost our baby…." She could say it now and somehow the words filled some of that emptiness that had yawned inside her for the past four years.

He nodded, his throat moving as he swallowed down his emotion. "And after. You had to deal with that *loss...*"

And they had lost more than the baby who'd been too undeveloped to survive her premature birth. The hysterectomy to stop the bleeding had ended the possibility of their having any other children together.

He swallowed hard. "You shouldn't have had to deal with all that pain—and unfounded guilt—all alone."

"You're here now," she pointed out, "with me." But holding each other wasn't enough anymore. Not with so much pain and passion between them.

His mouth moved over her face, kissing the curve of her cheek, the side of her nose before touching her lips. He kissed her gently, with a tenderness she hadn't felt from him in years, if ever. But then the passion, as always, ignited between them. She parted her lips, and he slid his tongue into her mouth, mating it with hers.

All their pain turned to passion, passion that had them clawing at each other's clothes. Ben pulled up her shirt and pushed down the cup of her bra so that his palm cupped her breast instead. Her nipple rubbed against his skin, peaked and sensitive.

She bit her lip and murmured. And reached for his fly, sliding her fingers up and down the hard ridge beneath his zipper. Then she parted the metal teeth and pushed aside cotton briefs so that his erection sprang free. She wrapped her hand around his cock and stroked the pulsing flesh.

"Paige," he growled against her lips—kissing her with heat and desperation before lowering his head to her breast. He nipped the point with his teeth before laving it with his tongue. And his hands were as busy as hers, moving up beneath her skirt and tugging aside her panties. His fingers slid inside her—in and out.

She threw back her head and bit her lip as a small orgasm shuddered through her. "You, I need you," she admitted. Not just now, but always, she feared.

But before she could react to her fear and pull back to protect herself—her heart—he lifted her. Instinctively she wrapped her legs around his waist and helped guide his cock inside her. They kissed, their mouths mating as their bodies did. He thrust deep, then deeper.

A pressure spiraled through her—so tight that she squirmed, then writhed. And came. He swallowed her scream, then groaned against her lips as he joined her in release, pumping hot and fast inside her.

He didn't release her—or separate from her—until he'd carried her into his private bathroom. While she cleaned up, he looked away—a muscle twitching along his jaw as if he'd had no release at all, as if something still gripped him.

Then she realized it was guilt. "I don't hate you," she told him again. "You must know that…."

After straightening his clothes, he walked back into his office and pushed his hand through his hair. "There's so much you don't know…so much you deserve to know."

"Are you finally going to tell me your secrets, Ben?" she asked.

"They're not my secrets to tell."

"I actually used to worry that there was another woman," she admitted.

He flinched as if she'd struck him. "I would never cheat on you. There's no one else."

"No one?"

"Not another woman." He lifted his hand to her face, brushing his fingertips across her cheek. "There's only you."

The ringing of her cell phone interrupted whatever else he'd been about to say. She reached for her purse, which had dropped from her shoulder onto the floor next to the desk, but Ben caught her hand. "Don't answer it. Let it go to voice mail."

"No, I need to get it. It could be…" Someone who would save her from facing any more pain, either from her past or from the future she couldn't have. "Kate. Maybe she knows who the stalker is."

She glanced at the caller ID window before opening the phone. "It's not Kate. It's Renae. Maybe she's looking for you. You left her your pager."

He sighed. "Answer it."

"Hello?"

"Paige?" The voice was thick with emotion and fear and barely recognizable. "I—I answered one of Ben's pages. I—I need to talk to him…."

Renae. But the trauma surgeon had never

sounded so rattled before. "What? What's going on?"

"It's Sebastian. It's bad! I need Ben...."

"Oh, my God!" She pressed a hand against her heart. "Has he been in an accident?"

"Paige, I need Ben. Only he knows what to do—"

His face tense with concern, Ben took the phone from her shaking hand. "Renae, tell me everything." He listened for a couple of seconds, then clicked off the phone.

"Ben!" She stared up at him, trying to read his face, but he wore the mask of someone uninvolved, unemotional. He'd looked like that the day he'd carried her bags out to her car and watched her drive away. "Ben?"

"I have to leave."

"He's here—in the hospital, right?" she asked. "He's hurt. It's bad—" From the look on his face, it was worse than she could imagine.

"He's not here. He's at the club."

"I'm going with you."

"You're risking your life, Paige," he warned her.

She wanted to ask how and a million other questions. But she didn't want to keep him from

Sebastian. It was his life that she was concerned about—not her own. "I don't care. I'm going with you!"

He stared at her—his eyes dark with so many emotions. He nodded, but then warned her, "I may not be able to save you both."

Chapter 15

Blood gushed from the stake pounded into Sebastian's chest. It squirted across the front of Renae's scrubs and sprayed her face. Despite being an experienced trauma surgeon, her hands trembled as she held the scalpel over her patient's bare chest.

"I've got it," Ben said as he assessed the situation, after rushing into the room. "Get cleaned up and get the *hell* out of here."

Her mouth fell open in shock. "But you need help."

He glanced around for Ingrid, but thank God his usual assistant wasn't around. Yet. She couldn't see a human inside the secret room.

"I've got it," he repeated. "You need to forget what happened. You need to forget that you were ever here."

"But—"

"Go," he shouted at her—so harshly that her eyes widened and the color drained from her face. Satisfied that she would now heed his warning, he turned back to Sebastian and concentrated on saving his friend. Again.

Please, God, let me save him again.

Last time Ben hadn't known he could fix a heart this damaged. He hadn't realized he possessed the skills necessary to reverse the trauma and the inescapable fate of a vampire with a stake through his heart.

Sebastian was supposed to die, according to the legend of the secret vampire society. A stake through the heart was the only way to kill an immortal.

Until Ben.

Sweat ran in his eyes as he worked, but he blinked away the moisture and focused. Thankful he'd equipped the room the same as a working O.R., he irrigated the wound. If he missed one splinter, an infection would kill Sebastian...if he survived at all.

"Dr. Davison..."

He speared a glance at the young trauma surgeon. "Get out of here!"

"Dr. Davison...Ben..." She clutched at his sleeve. "It's too late. He's lost so much blood. There's nothing else you can do for him."

"I can bring him back," he said, stating the unequivocal fact.

And she stared up at him like he was crazy until realization dawned. "You've done it before," she said. "I noticed the old scars on his chest."

"I can bring him back," he repeated as he continued to flush the wound. "I *have* to bring him back...."

"I know," she said, her breath catching. "He's Paige's brother. He's her *brother,* right?"

As well as the scar, she must have noticed the age of his organs. Ben remembered when he'd pieced it all together, when he'd pieced Sebastian together the first time.

"He's the only family she has," Ben said. "She can't lose him."

"Then let me help."

He glanced toward the other door, not the one open to the hall where he'd made Paige promise she would wait so she wasn't in his way when he treated Sebastian. He glanced toward the door that opened onto the sewer the secret society used as their private passageways to the Underground.

"You're risking your life just being here," he warned her, as he'd warned Paige earlier.

"If there's a chance of saving his…"

There had to be more than a chance. After their talk earlier that afternoon, Ben knew that Paige wouldn't be able to handle losing someone else she loved.

Paige's knees shook, but she forced herself to walk toward that room at the end of the hall, the one that was always locked. But now the door stood open. She couldn't keep her promise to Ben; she couldn't wait any longer for news of Sebastian's condition.

She fought hard against the threat of tears— even though her eyes were already swollen from crying. Over her dead daughter. Her dead marriage. Not over her brother. She had no tears left to cry over him. He could *not* die.

Ben had been working on him for more than an hour already. Over an hour she'd stood out in the hall, afraid for her brother's life and afraid to find out what had happened to him.

Everyone she'd ever cared about always left her. Was Sebastian going to leave her, too?

She had to find out, and so she pushed open the door the rest of way and stepped inside the secret room. She blinked in surprise at the bright lights, at the sterile environment of steel and cement. There were no rats, no sewer—only Ben and Renae working desperately on the man who lay on the metal O.R. table.

Sebastian had lied to her and Kate. Kate…

She should call the detective, should report… whatever the hell had happened here. Blood spattered Renae's scrubs. Paige would like to believe that wasn't Sebastian's blood—that Renae had gotten that way in the ER. But she'd been with her earlier.

And Renae hadn't brought with her the blood that pooled beneath the table on which Sebastian lied. More blood pumped into him through an IV.

"How is he?"

Renae glanced up, her eyes wide with dread and fear. And Paige knew.

Ben's gaze met hers, and the determination in his dark eyes eased some of her fear. "He's going to make it."

A gasp of surprise and doubt slipped through Renae's lips.

"He's going to make it," Ben vowed, holding Paige's gaze. "I promise you. He's going to make it."

His assurance didn't ease the tight knot of anxiety in Paige's stomach. Ben had made promises to her before that he hadn't kept.

"Don't give me hope if there is none," she warned him. Because it would only hurt that much more if she lost him...

The metal table creaked as Sebastian's body tensed, then convulsed.

"He's coming around!" Renae shrieked—with even more surprise than she'd had for Ben's pledge. "I thought he was dead. No human could survive an injury like that...."

"An injury like what?" But as Paige asked it, she arrived at the answer herself as she noticed the bloody stake on Ben's instrument tray.

A human would not have been able to survive a stake through the heart. But neither should a vampire.

Ben injected something into Sebastian's IV, something that stopped the convulsions. "Paige, you and Renae need to get out of here. Now!"

"But you need help," Renae insisted.

"I've got it now," Ben said as he continued to work on Sebastian's open chest. "You two need to leave this room before dark. No one can know you've been back here—that you know."

Paige wished she didn't know—that she hadn't put it all together. Even though everything suddenly made sense, it was so incredible—so surreal.

"I can't leave him."

"You have to," Ben insisted. "He wouldn't want you here. He wouldn't want you to get hurt."

"But how?"

"It's a secret no human can learn."

"But you know…." And he'd obviously known for a while but hadn't shared it with her.

"Because they need me, they let me live…."

Renae shuddered, drawing their attention.

"Get your friend out of here," Ben told Paige. "She has nothing to do with any of this. You don't want her getting hurt, too."

Her hand trembling, she grabbed Renae's arm and tugged her from the room. With one last glance at the man she'd believed to be her younger brother, she closed the door behind herself. *He'll be all right,* she assured herself, but…nothing would ever be the same.

As he closed the wound in Sebastian's chest, Ben breathed a sigh of relief. "You're going to be fine, my friend," he said. This was one promise to Paige that Ben could keep.

Sebastian shifted against the metal table again—not in convulsions but as if he were awakening. From the last time he'd treated the vampire, Ben knew that anesthesia didn't work with him. It didn't keep him unconscious. Nor did it dull the pain. The vampire felt everything.

"I wish I could do more for you."

Sebastian's fingers flexed, reaching out. Ben took his hand. "Take your time. Rest."

Giving orders to Sebastian was an exercise in futility.

"Gotta tell you…" Sebastian murmured, his voice a hoarse rasp. He licked his lips. "Gotta…"

"You recover quickly," Ben reminded him with awe in the speed with which vampires recuperated—no matter the severity of their injuries. "When you get stronger, you'll tell me what the hell happened."

Metal creaked, and he glanced toward the door. It remained closed and locked; he'd locked it behind Paige and the young trauma surgeon. He lifted his gaze toward the security monitor and confirmed that the hall was empty. But the metal creaked louder and he whirled around to the other door.

"I'm too late," Ingrid observed as she stepped into the secret room from the Underground passageways.

"For what?" Ben asked as he assessed Sebastian's vitals, which were rapidly improving. He would keep his promise to Paige; he had to.

"I'm too late to help you save him." She walked around the room, studying the blood and the discarded instruments. "Who helped you?"

"No one," Ben lied.

The dark-haired vampiress gestured toward his patient. "You didn't do this alone."

"Yeah, I did," he insisted. "It wasn't that bad."

Her hand steady, when even the young trauma surgeon's had trembled, she picked up the blood-soaked wooden stake. "It was bad."

"He's tough." Ben was counting on it—was

counting on Sebastian recovering as quickly and completely as he had last time someone had driven a stake through his heart.

"That's not the adjective that comes to mind when I think of Sebastian," Ingrid said, her fingers tightening around the stake. "'Reckless' is. And he's so reckless that he puts us all at risk."

"He's the one who's hurt," Ben pointed out. "He's the one fighting for his life."

Ingrid shook her head. "No. He's not."

Ben leaned closer to his patient, whose lashes fluttered as his eyes opened. "He's doing better," he said, allowing himself a satisfied grin.

But Sebastian's eyes—the same bright blue as his daughter's—widened with panic and fear.

To assure all of them, Ben added, "He's going to be just fine."

But his friend's gaze left his to fixate on a point over Ben's shoulder.

"I wasn't talking about Sebastian," Ingrid clarified for him.

Then something sharp but too thin for a stake or a fang, pierced the skin on Ben's neck. Wincing against the sting, he started to lift his hand to check the wound, but his muscles trembled, then numbed. And he dropped to the floor.

"You're the one who needs to fight for his life, Dr. Davison," Ingrid advised in her creepy, husky voice.

But Ben couldn't fight. She'd given him an injection of the paralyzing drug. At least he would feel no pain....

And he didn't when she attacked. He felt no physical pain, but emotionally he ached for Paige. Just as she'd accused him, he always left her.

This time he worried that he wouldn't be able to come back to her. This time he feared was the last time he would ever leave Paige.

Chapter 16

Paige tried the handle for the door at the end of the hall, but the knob didn't turn. When Ben had convinced her and Renae to leave a few hours ago, she had only shut it; she hadn't locked it behind herself. Ben must have locked her out of his life again.

She should have been used to his pushing her away, but pain and anger gripped her. Willing to fight now, she fisted her hands and banged on the door. "Let me in! Damn it—let me in!"

Had he broken another promise? Had Ben lost Sebastian?

Tears stung her eyes, and she pounded harder. She had a right to know *everything*. "Let me in!"

If Sebastian had died…

The knob turned and metal hinges creaked as finally the door opened. And Sebastian stood before her, his chest swaddled with bandages.

"H-how…?" Was it possible that he was already up and on his feet when just hours ago he'd been impaled with a stake through his heart? "Are you okay?"

He pushed his hand through his tangled, sweat-dampened hair. "Yeah, yeah…"

Doubting him—as she should have when he'd first showed back up in her life—she glanced behind him, looking for his doctor to confirm or deny her broth—Sebastian's claim. "Where's Ben?"

"Gone," he replied, a muscle twitching in his cheek.

"He left you alone?" She shouldn't have been surprised. "He shouldn't have."

"I'm fine," he said, and as if to prove the point, he joined her in the hall and closed the door behind himself, hiding all the blood and medical paraphernalia from her sight.

"You're not fine," she said as she steered him toward the office, where he dropped onto the leather sofa. "I saw what happened to you. I can't believe you're alive."

"I'm sorry, Paige," he said.

"For what?" she asked, opening her eyes to meet his gaze. "For lying to me or for scaring me half to death?"

"You know who I am?"

Biting her lip, she nodded.

"Then you know *what* I am," he said with a ragged sigh. "That's why I couldn't stick around. I couldn't risk anyone figuring it out."

"Because no human can know and live," she said, repeating what Ben had told her. "But I was just a little girl. I wouldn't have figured it out."

"Your mother would have," he pointed out. "And you needed her."

"I needed you."

Mom had done her best, but the woman had never had the most prudent judgment.

"I was around, Paige. You just didn't see me…."

She shivered, remembering those times she'd

awakened, feeling as though someone had been watching her sleep. "The money..."

He nodded.

The envelopes of cash had shown up when she'd needed them most—for food, for rent, for school.... "I thought it was you—that it had to be you."

He sighed. "It wasn't enough."

"No," she agreed. "So why did you come back to me? I was older, taking care of myself. I didn't need you then."

He nodded. "You did. You just didn't know it."

She shook her head, her anger returning. "Or did you need something I had? You needed Ben."

"I didn't know that then. I didn't know that Ben would be able to reverse a legacy." He pushed his hand through his hair again, and this time his fingers trembled. "I just knew that someone had made a threat...about you."

"No." She shook her head again. "I've never had anyone bother me until I bought this place." She shuddered, knowing now what all her patrons were. Not just beautiful and not actually young...

"She wasn't really after you. The stalker was *mine*—then and now," he said, his breath rattling in his bandaged chest, as his eyes filled with guilt and misery. "She was threatening you because of *me*."

"*She?* Who's she?" The question slipped out. Paige really didn't want to interrogate him now; he wasn't as recovered as she'd initially thought.

"A woman I dated a lifetime ago." He coughed, then grimaced.

She crossed to the couch and dropped to her knees before him. "Seb—" She wasn't certain what to call him now that she knew who he really was. But she couldn't call this man—who looked younger than she was, this man she'd considered her brother, her father. "Sebastian, shhh…"

"I'm so, so sorry, Paige."

She reached for his hand, holding it in both of hers. "Don't get worked up."

"It was *my* fault," he said, his fingers clutching at hers.

She shook her head. "No, you didn't bring this on—no matter what you did." He was a playboy; she'd thought he'd taken after their father in that respect. But it wasn't genetic; it was just habit.

"I didn't know she had problems," he said, "when I started seeing her. I didn't realize how dangerous she was."

"She could have killed you." She swallowed hard, choking on emotion. He might have left her forever this time. "She *intended* to kill you."

"I thought she was gone," he said, "after she attacked me the last time years ago. I didn't think she'd come back again."

"Where is she now?"

His shoulders lifted in a shrug, and he grimaced. "I don't know."

"We need to call Kate and report your attack like Renae wanted to."

Sebastian grimaced again. "Oh, God, Renae… I thought I was paging Ben."

"I don't know how you managed to page anyone," she said. "You should have called the police instead of Ben."

He sighed. "I would have called anyone… but Renae."

"Then let's call the police now," she suggested, "I should have called Kate earlier, when Renae wanted to, but I had no idea what was going on."

"You shouldn't know—you can't know what I am, what happened—"

"I was with Ben when Renae called him," she explained. "I knew you were hurt."

Sebastian squeezed her hands. "You should have stayed away. Ben saved me." He sighed. "Again."

"But she's still out there," she reminded him. "She could and probably will try again. Kate needs to find her before she does."

"No," he said, and squeezed her hands so tightly that she winced. "You'll get your friend killed. This society—it has its own laws and rules. It doesn't abide by the laws of mortals. Kate has no authority Underground."

"Who does?" she asked, then wondered aloud, "Ben?" She'd noticed how every one of her patrons had seemed to know and respect him. She hadn't suspected anything amiss then because Dr. Davison was a world-renowned cardiologist. She hadn't realized it wasn't just this world. "Is that why he's allowed to live even though he's a mortal who knows the secret?"

"No, no, not Ben," Sebastian weakly protested.

"He can't help?"

"No, he can't." That muscle twitched in his jaw again as he clenched it tightly.

His reaction had the hair rising on the nape of Paige's neck. "Has something happened to Ben?"

"He's gone."

"I know—he's not here. Why isn't he here?" He might have left *her* over the years, but Ben had never left a patient who obviously still needed him.

"The Ben you love," Sebastian continued as if she hadn't spoken, "is *gone*."

She stared at him, trying to understand what he meant. Then she noted the tears glittering in the depths of his eyes, and she got it. As if someone had driven a stake through her heart, pain pierced it, and she doubled over.

Sebastian closed his eyes, trying to shut out his daughter's anguish—and his own guilt. "I'm so sorry, Paige. I've made such a mess of your life. I never should have come back."

"You thought I was in danger," she reminded him. "But it was you…and Ben who got hurt."

If he hadn't come back, though, if he hadn't taken that stake all those years ago, *she* might have. And being human, she wouldn't have survived an injury like that. Ben wouldn't have been able to save *her.*

"I should have left," he said, "when I got better. I should have taken off then, since she was gone. But, when he saved me, Ben had figured out the secret. And knowing it put him in danger."

A sob slipped through Paige's quivering lips. "Obviously…"

"I was there. I saw it, but I was still too weak to help him." He'd known Ben was in danger and had been trying to warn him…but he hadn't realized that Ingrid was the threat.

He shuddered. "All these times he's helped me, and I did nothing for him." But lay there and watch it happen. "I'm sorry, Paige."

Because of him, she'd lost the man she loved all over again.

Lifting his fingers to his neck, Ben probed the fang marks. It hadn't just been a nightmare.

"Why'd you do it?" he asked Ingrid, who stood in the shadows of his bedroom. She'd brought him back to his house, probably through the Underground tunnels. Being a vampiress, she was superhuman strong. No, just strong—she wasn't human at all. And now thanks to her, neither was he.

"I had to."

He shook his head, which was just a weak turn of his neck so that it shifted against the pillow.

"To protect you," she explained. "That little speech you gave a few nights ago, threatening us to stay away from your ex, pissed off a lot of people."

"What happened to Sebastian had nothing to do with my speech. It was her…that woman who came after him a decade ago."

Ingrid's dark eyes widened with horror. "*She* came back? That crazy woman?"

Pot meet kettle. After what she'd done to him, the vampiress had no right to criticize another member of the society. But Ben held back his anger. He'd already proved no match for Ingrid's madness.

"Yeah, and she's still out there. So he's still in danger." And so probably was Paige, since the woman's threats against her had been what had brought Sebastian back to his daughter.

"She got away?"

Ben nodded. "Just like last time. She was gone before I got there." He didn't even know what this woman looked like.

"And if she comes back sooner, to finish what she tried doing to him, I might be too weak to help him." Or Paige. "If something happens again—" he could lift his arm now, could move, yet his muscles were still slack, still too weak for him to fight "—to anyone, I'm useless. You shouldn't have done this to me."

"I know what I'm doing," Ingrid insisted. "You're going to be fine. You'll be stronger than you've ever been. You'll be immortal."

"I've worked on humans who've been turned," he reminded her. "I lost most of them. The blood loss destroyed their organs. It's too dangerous."

The vampiress shook her head, too stubborn and irrational to listen to what he was saying—to concede that he could be right and she wrong. "No, it's more dangerous for you to be human."

"Being one of you won't protect me from a stake through the heart," he reminded her. "I'm the only one who can protect you—who can save you from that."

"And that's why you need to be one of us—you need to be immortal," she explained, as if he were the one who had no grasp on reality, "or there will come a time when you're too old, too feeble to help us."

He raised his hand and tried to curl his fingers into a fist. "I'm feeble now. I couldn't hold a scalpel. I couldn't save anyone now."

Not even himself.

"You'll be fine," she assured him again. "You just need to replenish the blood you've lost."

"I've lost more than blood."

"Your wife."

"Ex." He would have to think of Paige that way now.

"You won't have a future with her," she said, "because eventually, as she ages and you don't, she'll figure out the secret."

Now the secret was his to keep, too. But Paige had already figured it out. And if he had anything to do with her anymore, she would also figure out that he was now part of that secret—part of the society.

"As long as you make sure nothing happens to her, I'll stay away from her," he promised.

Ingrid arched her dark brows with surprise. "I thought that you were still in love with her."

It was because he loved her so much that he would stay away. "Her being safe is more important than my being with her," he said, his heart as heavy as his still partially paralyzed limbs.

"You really do love her," Ingrid said with a wistful sigh.

"I love her enough to let her go." Finally.

Chapter 17

"I knew you'd show up here eventually," Paige said. And she had known that now it would have to be after dark.

Ben's long, lean body tensed, and he straightened away from the bed where the little girl slept. "What are you doing here?" he asked, without turning toward her. "Visiting hours ended a while ago."

She uncurled herself from the chair where she had dozed off. "I was waiting for you." And she'd been playing cards with Addi until the child had fallen asleep.

He drew in an audibly shaky breath and shook his head. "You shouldn't have."

"I had to make sure you were all right," she explained, her heart constricting with the fear she'd had for him. "Sebastian told me what happened to you."

"How is he?"

Of course he'd worry about his patient first, himself last. That was why she'd been so certain he would show up to check on Addi.

"He's still a little weak." Remembering what Sebastian had been through, she couldn't believe he was even alive. "But he's recovering with unbelievable speed."

"Good, that's good."

She reached out to touch Ben, but he pulled back and she withdrew her hand. "Are you?"

"I'm…" He closed his eyes and flinched.

But she doubted his pain was physical now… despite the bandage on his neck. "I know."

He shook his head. "You *can't* know."

"Mama," the little girl murmured in her sleep as she shifted against her pillow.

Paige flinched now, with the reminder that no

child of hers would ever call her mother. And she couldn't have a surrogate bring a baby into the world that she now knew existed. "I know," she repeated, once Addi, with a wistful little sigh, had settled back to sleep, "and I should have known a long time ago."

Ben shook his head in denial.

Anger raised her voice. "You should have told me."

He caught her arm, his grip strong. As he ushered her out of the room and down the hall to the elevator, his strength reassured her even as his silence unsettled her and had her trembling slightly. He didn't speak until the elevator stopped on the office level.

"Are you afraid of me now?" he asked. "Now that you know what I've become?"

"I've never been afraid of you," she said.

She had only been afraid of what she'd felt for him. Too much. She'd never wanted to be dependent on a man, the way her mother had been.

He released his hold on her to unlock the door that opened directly into his private office. "You didn't have a reason to fear me before." He shut the door behind her and locked it. "You do now." His eyes glowed eerily in the dark. "I'm one of them. I'm a monster now."

Ben had never been more attractive to her. The silver strands glittered in his dark hair, like the desire in his dark eyes. Always lean and muscular, he seemed taller now—stronger now.

"No," she said. "You're not a monster."

"Sebastian told you—I've been turned."

"It wasn't your choice. One of them attacked you." Probably so they wouldn't lose him as she had.

"But I'm consigned now to this life of darkness." The light left his eyes now as he squeezed them shut and passed a hand over them. "I can't and I won't ask you to share this life with me."

"You *never* let me share your life," Paige reminded him.

"It was just…after I learned the secret," he insisted. "I couldn't risk your figuring it out, too. They wouldn't let you live if you learned about them…about me."

She shook her head. "It was even before then. From the day we met, you always held a part of yourself back from me."

"I did. I know I did." His breath shuddered out

in a sigh. "I think I did it to protect myself—because every time in my past that I got attached to someone, I had to leave."

"You didn't *have* to leave me," she said, her heart aching as she remembered all those times he'd walked away from her. "You *chose* to leave me."

His broad shoulders lifted in a shrug, muscles rippling beneath the thin cashmere of his charcoal-gray sweater. "Leaving was all I knew."

"Me, too," she reminded him. "All I knew was getting left."

"Sebastian had to leave you," he said, defending her father. "If he'd stuck around, people would have noticed that he never aged. He left you to protect you. He loves you."

"That's not why you left me," she said. He hadn't been one of them then, but he still hadn't wanted her close. "Did you ever really love me?"

"Paige, I loved you."

"*Loved* me?" she asked, a pang striking her heart. "You don't anymore?"

He drew in a breath, as if to brace himself, and said, "I can't."

"So your mind is made up. You don't want me

in this life of yours, either," she realized. "So why did you bother bringing me to your office? There was obviously no point in our talking." Maybe that was why she, a lawyer, had never tried arguing with him when they'd been married. Back then, Ben had been too strong, too resolute, for her to break down that wall he'd built around himself. Now he was even stronger.

"I didn't bring you here to talk," Ben admitted. "I brought you here for..." He moved away from the door, closing the distance between them with one long stride.

Her pulse tripped, and she trembled slightly. "What? For what did you bring me here?"

"One." He reached out. "Last." His fingers deftly unbuttoned the small buttons of her blouse and pulled it from her shoulders. "Time."

She should have summoned the pride that had held her back from admitting she'd been fired from the law firm. But her pride was damned; all she felt was desire.

Her heart raced as he pulled her closer, his hands on her hips, dragging her tight against his hard body. She rose up on tiptoe and nipped at his chin.

"One last time?" She needed this; she needed

him. "You think you can manage that? That I can?" She smiled and reminded him, "We've never been able to stay away from each other."

"It has to be the *last* time. I can't stay in your life," he insisted, but his eyes were intense and dark with passion, his body taut and hot against hers.

"I don't want to fight," she said, pressing her mouth to his. But she would fight for him; she wouldn't let him lock himself away in the Underground—no matter that he was now one of them.

And if she'd doubted what Sebastian had told her, she had proof now as she slid her tongue between his lips and over the sharp point of a fang.

He pulled back. "Sorry…"

But she grasped the nape of his neck and tugged his head down to hers again. And she kissed him with all the passion she always had. She wasn't afraid of the fangs. She knew he would never hurt her. Physically.

Emotionally. She'd deal with that later….

His hands slid from her hips to cup her buttocks. He fisted her skirt in his hands, lifting it as he lifted her against him. She wrapped her legs around his waist, and her arms around his neck.

He reached between them to unbutton and unzip his pants. Then he pushed her panties aside, first with his fingers, then the wet tip of his cock. "Paige…"

She slid down, over the length of him, taking him deep inside her. "Ben…"

He groaned, then dragged her tank top, which she'd worn with the sheer blouse, up and off. Since the camisole had a built-in bra, she'd worn nothing beneath it. He groaned again, then leaned over and pulled one of her nipples into his mouth, laving the sensitive point with his tongue. Then the tip of a fang scraped over her skin.

"Oh…" She moaned at the wicked sensation.

She arched her back and moved her hips, shifting so that he drove deeper. Each thrust brought her closer…the passion built inside her. His mouth on her breast pulled, sending heat streaking through her. He reached between them, pushing his thumb against her clit until she came, her orgasm crashing over him.

She buried her face in his neck, gasping for breath. But he didn't stop. He stumbled a couple of steps until her bare back came up against the wall. Then he drove harder, deeper, each thrust lifting her up.

She splayed her arms, bracing herself against the wainscoting of his office wall. Her back arched. His mouth moved along her neck, his fangs scraping the skin as he sucked her flesh. But he didn't bite—although she sensed the urge in him. Instead he slid his mouth over her collarbone and back to her breasts. Again he drew a sensitive peak into his mouth. A fang scraped the nipple, heightening the pressure until it broke free. And tears of pleasure streaked from her eyes.

"Ben!"

"Come again, Paige," he ordered her, his mouth against her breast.

She tugged on his hair, to pull him closer, not away. As he nipped at her—the fangs just scraping but not breaking through the skin, she came again, shattering in his arms.

He thrust once, twice then shouted her name, "Paige!"

She unwrapped her legs and slid down his body, trembling with the aftermath of their passion. Naked and more vulnerable than she'd ever been, she reached for her clothes.

But he caught her wrists and pulled her hands away until they dropped back to her sides. Then his fingertips moved across her skin, along the scratches his fangs had left on her. "Paige, I'm so sorry. I never meant to be so rough."

"You weren't," she assured. "You didn't hurt me."

"But I would." He tensed and clenched his jaw, a muscle leaping in his cheek. "Because of what I am, I would…"

She shook her head. "No, you wouldn't. You didn't hurt me."

He lifted his fingertips, stained with a faint streak of blood that had trickled from one of the scratches. "I have and I would—"

"That's nothing," she said, dismissing the blood.

He shook his head. "I know what they're capable of…what I'm capable of. This was the *last* time."

That was all this had been; she realized now that he'd spoken the truth. And no matter how much he loved her—or maybe because he loved her, he was going to walk away from her again. And she doubted she could fight hard enough to get him to return to her.

"You didn't have to walk me back here," Paige said, "especially seeing as how you intend to stay away from me from now on."

"I have to," Ben reminded her, and himself. He never should have touched her. One last time. It wasn't enough. He wanted more—he always wanted more with Paige.

Even now he tasted her on his lips, the sweet flavor of her blood. He'd nearly sunk his fangs into her neck, nearly drank of her essence. His control had held barely. This time. He couldn't trust that if there was a next time, he'd be able to control his new dark desires.

"I could find my purse on my own," she said as they neared Addi's room. "I think it's just under the chair."

"I need to check on her," he explained. Paige had distracted him from doing that earlier. He also needed to make sure that Paige got safely home—since the sun had hours before it rose.

"H-how are you going to handle your career now?" she asked.

He blew out a ragged breath. "I don't know…."

"You can't give it up," she said.

"You gave up being a lawyer."

"I got fired," she reminded him.

"And you could have got another job at any

law firm in Zantrax," he pointed out. "Or you could have started your own practice."

"I could have," she agreed.

"Then why didn't you?" he asked.

"I thought we weren't talking anymore," she said as she slipped inside the room.

The hair lifted on Ben's nape with foreboding. Even before he joined her, he knew they weren't alone. Someone stood in the shadows of the little girl's private hospital room. Addi lay in her bed, her skin paler than he'd ever seen it.

"There's something wrong with her," Paige said as she leaned over the child's bed. "She's barely breathing." Then she lifted her head to the person lurking in the shadows, and a scream escaped her lips.

Ben covered Paige's mouth, not wanting anyone else drawn to the room—anyone else hurt. "What did you do?" he asked Addi's mother. But she was so much more than just a patient's mother.

The vampiress met his gaze across her daughter's bed. "I did what you couldn't, *Doctor.* I made certain that she will never die."

Paige's breath escaped in a gasp against his palm.

"You turned her?" Ben asked, dread filling him.

"I—I had to…." She pushed a bloodstained hand through her hair. "I didn't want her to die."

"But you wanted Sebastian to die," Ben said.

"You saved him?" She laughed. "I knew I should have killed you first. Then you wouldn't have been able to help him. But then, if you were dead, you wouldn't have been able to help my Adelaide if she needed you." She smoothed her fingers over her daughter's forehead, streaking the pale skin with blood. "She doesn't need you anymore."

"Miss Plumb—Marissa, this is a bad idea," Ben said. "She's not strong enough…to survive being turned. She just had surgery."

"And it didn't help."

"You just needed to give her time to heal. It takes longer for…" He couldn't say *us,* but he couldn't bring himself to say *them,* either. "She's human."

"She's not anymore," her mother said with great satisfaction.

"She may not be anything anymore," Ben said, his voice cracking as emotion overwhelmed him. "She's not strong enough, Marissa."

"You're not strong enough," she said. "And neither is she." She gestured at Paige. "You can't fight me off."

"You're wrong," Ben said as he pulled Paige away from the bed and thrust her behind him. "I'm not human anymore. I've been turned."

Marissa shook her head. "No…"

"I'm a vampire, too," Ben said, nearly choking on the declaration as he made it aloud for the first time.

"It doesn't matter," she said. "You can't operate on yourself. You won't be able to change your own legacy. And you won't be able to change *his* when I finally get rid of him for good."

"You attacked Sebastian," Ben deduced. "This time and the last time it was you." He glanced to the little girl in the bed and realized why Addi reminded him so much of Paige. "She's his daughter."

"She's *my* daughter."

"You don't deserve her," Paige said, able to speak now since Ben's hand no longer covered her mouth. "She deserves more than you."

"You," Marissa snarled at them. "You're the only one he cared about. I'm glad it's working

out this way. That I'm going to kill you first."
She flew at them, over her daughter's bed, a
stake clutched in her bloody hands.

Ben blocked Paige with his body and lifted
his arms to thwart off the attack. Having just
been turned, he wasn't as strong as Marissa was.
Not only was she strong, but she was also out of
her mind with madness. Even crazier than
Ingrid....

Ben didn't have her strength, but he had
something more powerful to use in this fight.
Love. This time he would protect Paige—or die
trying.

Chapter 18

A scream burned Paige's throat, but she was afraid to utter it. She didn't want to draw anyone else into the room and risk his or her safety; nor did she want to wake the sleeping child, if Addi actually could awaken.

Had her mother killed her?

She'd heard that fear in Ben's voice—the fear that echoed in his grunts as he grappled with the crazy vampiress. His hands locked around her wrists, holding the sharpened point of the stake away from his chest.

The scream threatened to slip free—not out of fear for herself but for Ben. She could not keep losing him—especially not like this. This time would be permanent. No one could repair the damage that stake would do to his heart. Renae hadn't been able to save Sebastian without Ben's help; she wouldn't be able to save Ben.

As the only human in this fight, Paige had no idea what to do. She just cowered behind him as he fought—not for his life but for hers. Because she wasn't one of them—of that damn secret society—she was helpless to fight them. She could not match their strength. But she could find someone who would help—someone, she suspected, who had always been there for her whether she'd known it or not.

Slipping from behind Ben, Paige ran for the door. But the woman was there, vaulting over them to block the exit with her body. "Where are *you* going?"

"Please, let us go," she beseeched her.

"You need to die first," the woman said, her eyes glowing with madness. "You're the only thing he ever loved." Her nails like talons, she reached for Paige.

But Ben jerked Paige back, with such force that she fell onto the floor behind him. "You don't want to hurt her," he said. "You want to hurt me."

"No, she wants to hurt me," a deep voice murmured.

Suddenly Sebastian was there—as if he'd slipped through a window. He stood over Paige, protecting her—as she realized he always had.

The vampiress snorted with derision. "Of course you would come out of hiding to protect *her.*"

"I wasn't hiding," he said.

"Then why were you never there for me…for her?" With the hand clutching the stake, she gestured toward the child lying on the bed.

Sebastian glanced at the little girl, and a gasp slipped from his lips. "She's mine?"

"No! She's mine!" Marissa screamed. "You're not going to take her from me!" And she lunged toward the bed with the stake.

But Sebastian, despite the injury he'd suffered, was quicker than she was. He caught the stake in his hand, holding it back from striking his child's heart.

Marissa turned on him, flying at him. He wasn't strong enough to simply knock the stake from her hand. He held it off, as Ben had, his fingers locked around her wrist. "Get her out of here," he yelled at them.

While Paige struggled to understand who he meant, Ben reached for the little girl and lifted her from the bed. One arm wrapped around the child, he extended his other hand to Paige and dragged her to her feet. Then he pulled her along behind him down the darkened hall.

"We can't leave him...alone with her," Paige protested, turning back toward the room. An eerie flash of light burst through the doorway, along with an inhuman scream.

"Now," Ben said, urging her faster. Instead of jumping into the open elevator, he pushed open the door to the stairs. "Hold on to me."

She wrapped her arms around his waist, holding tight as he vaulted up—instead of down—the steps. His feet didn't even touch the metal treads, and as he burst through the door to the roof, he launched into the air.

Paige fought down another scream—of fear and surprise. Ben really wasn't the man she'd known any longer. He was one of them.

* * *

"Is she okay?" Paige asked as he joined her in the dark garden behind Ben's house. She hadn't even glanced up, but yet she'd somehow known he was there.

He wondered if she'd ever be able to look at him again after what she'd witnessed. Feeling his fangs had been one thing, now she'd experienced the entire reality of his new existence.

"Addi? Yes, I think she'll be all right."

"I thought you were going to bring her to that secret room…." She shuddered. "The one at the club."

Despite everything that had happened and the nightmare he was now living, Ben's lips curved into a faint smile. "That's why I couldn't bring her there. She's just a little girl. Now she will always be a little girl."

"What?" She finally turned to him, her brow furrowed with confusion.

"That's what happens," he explained. "They don't age from the moment they're turned. Now she will always be nine years old."

Tears glittered in her eyes. "How could that woman do that to her own daughter?" She lifted a trembling hand to her mouth. "What about Sebastian? What did she do to him?"

"He's fine," Ben assured her.

"He wasn't hurt?"

"No." Not physically. Emotionally, Ben doubted his friend would ever be the same. Sebastian had spent the past several centuries as a lover; he had never been a fighter. Until tonight. But then he'd never had as much to fight for. "He's in there, sitting with Addi."

Paige nodded. "She's his daughter? My sister. No wonder she looked so much how I imagined—"

"Our baby would have looked had she lived?"

Paige sucked in a breath and pressed her hand against her heart.

"I had no idea how much you were still hurting until you told me." He grimaced, hurting for her and himself, for all they had lost. "I should have known."

"How?" she asked. "I wouldn't talk to you about it…about her."

And that explained why she'd wanted only fun and games and sex—and nothing serious between them anymore. Because she hadn't wanted to think about their child.

"I should have known," he said with another grimace, of pain instead of regret this time, "because I still hurt for her, too. But I want you to know, Paige, that I never blamed you."

"I thought you did," she said, reminding him of the guilt she'd shouldered alone. "I thought that's why you didn't fight the divorce."

"The secret—"

"You didn't let me go just over the secret," she said, a lawyer arguing her case.

He sighed, weary from more than lack of sleep. "I wanted to give you what you wanted, Paige."

"I couldn't have what I wanted. She died." Her breath shuddered out in a sob. "What did they do with her after she died?"

Paige had nearly died, too, so she'd been unconscious during the C-section and in and out of consciousness for days afterward. Ben had had to deal with the death of their daughter alone, but he was used to dealing alone.

"I had her cremated."

"Did you…name her?"

He nodded again as he blinked back the threat of tears. He'd never cried over their daughter.

"Ben?" Her voice cracked with the emotions clawing at her. "What did you call her?"

"The name we'd agreed on for a girl."

"Penelope."

"Penny," he said. He'd warned her when she'd brought up the name, that he would never call her Penelope, at least not as a baby. The name was too big. Penny was better. Since she'd never be anything other than a baby, Penny was perfect.

She dashed away some tears with the back of her hand. "What did you do with Penny's... ashes?"

Ben took her hand and led her deeper into the dark garden, toward the small koi pond they'd put in the backyard, in the middle of the evergreen garden. A tiny fountain in the shape of a cement angel spewed water into an arc that reflected those streaks of pink and purple light breaking over the horizon.

Those streaks were a warning that he needed to go inside soon, before the sun rose. But he couldn't leave Paige and their daughter alone.

"You put her in the pond?"

He gestured toward one of the stones on the side, to the bronze plaque riveted to its surface. Penelope "Penny" Culver-Davison, 2006, Precious Baby, Eternal Angel.

She ran her fingers over the engraving in the

bronze plate. "Penny…" Then she rose up on tiptoe and pressed her lips against Ben's cheek. "Thank you. For taking care of her…."

"I wish…" He swallowed hard, choking on his regrets and the desire that clutched at him over her nearness. "I wish I'd taken care of you. That I'd been there for you more."

"We can't go back and change the past," she pointed out.

"And we have no future."

"We could…"

He shook his head. "You know—you've experienced it—that I'm one of them."

"Make me one of them, too," she implored him. "Then we can share a life—the way we're finally sharing our loss."

His heart constricted. "Paige, you don't know what you're asking."

"I know that everyone I care about is part of this society. You, my sister, my…*father*…"

"Your friends," he pointed out, "aren't part of it. They can't learn of it. You'd have to give them up before they caught on."

"They were there for me…." she murmured, her gaze drawn again to the bronze plaque and the pennies sparkling in the bottom of the pond.

"They were there for you when I wasn't," he said. "They stood by you. Can you leave them…like I may have to leave one day?"

She sucked in an audible breath. "You're leaving?"

"Members of the society can't stay in one place very long—not without risking others learning the secret. They have to move around. You can't," he pointed out. "You have a life here."

"So do you," she said. "You have a career."

"I can be a doctor in other cities, other countries—anywhere," he pointed out.

"So you're going to leave?" she asked, her voice hoarse with pain. "And Sebastian and Addi?"

"They'll have to leave, too," he admitted. "Sebastian should have left years ago. You were already remarking how he never ages. Other people will have noticed that, too."

"But he stayed for me," she said, her eyes warm with love for the father she had spent most of her life resenting. "To keep me safe from that woman."

"She's gone now," Ben revealed. "You have nothing to fear from her. But your knowledge of the secret risks your life. You need to leave." He glanced toward the lightening sky. "And I need to get inside."

"Ben…" She grasped his arm, holding on. "Please, let me stay with you. Forever."

The temptation pulled at him, but he shook his head and shook off her hand. "I can't…"

He had no idea how he would endure eternity without her, but he couldn't hurt her anymore. He'd already hurt her too much.

Paige stepped inside her empty condo, and the loneliness consumed her. They were all going to leave her; she should have been used to it. Yet she couldn't imagine a life without Ben in it.

She had no more than kicked off her shoes than the doorbell rang behind her. He'd changed his mind. Her hands shaking, she pulled open the door. "Ben—"

But it wasn't Ben. Kate pushed her way inside. "Okay, tell me what the hell's going on!"

"I don't know what you mean," she replied, stalling, then closed the door behind her irate friend. Had Renae called the detective, after all?

"You're being stalked but I haven't heard from you in days. I've been scared as hell that something happened to you," Kate explained.

"I'm fine," Paige lied.

Her eyes narrowed, Kate studied her as she

probably studied the face of suspects. Finally, after a few long moments, she sighed. "You're not going to tell me the truth."

"There's nothing to tell."

"That scar on your neck tells another story," Kate said.

Paige lifted her fingers to the mostly healed wound. It must have been Marissa that night in the dark. "It's over…"

"What—how?" Kate asked. "You found out who your stalker is?"

Paige nodded.

"Ben?"

"God, no!"

Kate released a sigh of relief; maybe the detective wasn't so cynical, after all. Or maybe the friend had just known how much Paige loved him. "Then who?"

"A woman who was involved with Sebastian." A lifetime ago. "She was really after him."

"I need to talk to him, then," Kate said. "Is he here?"

Sun streamed through the tall windows, shining off the polished hardwood floor. "No. But it's over."

"What do you mean?"

"She's not going to be a problem anymore." Ben hadn't said, but Paige knew that the woman was dead, because if Marissa was still a threat, Ben wouldn't have pushed Paige away again. "She's gone."

"For now. But what if she comes back?"

Paige shook her head. "She won't. They finally worked things out."

"But she's dangerous. Look at what she did to you."

Paige closed her eyes, remembering what Marissa had done to Sebastian. The vampiress had been far more dangerous than Kate realized.

"I'm fine," she insisted.

"Why do I think you're lying to me?"

Because Kate was a brilliant detective and an even better friend.

Paige forced a smile. "I've just had a long night. I'm tired."

"You weren't at the club."

The club. Who had Sebastian left in charge when he'd come to her rescue at the hospital? "You were there?"

"It was packed, but I couldn't find you," Kate said. "I tried getting into that room again to see if you were in there."

Paige held her breath. If Kate had gotten inside…

"First damn lock that I haven't been able to pick," Kate admitted.

"That's a good thing."

Kate lifted a brow.

Paige shuddered with relief. "I don't want you releasing sewer rats into the club."

"I think they'd be more frightened to mingle with some of your patrons," Kate said. "That's a tough crowd."

The detective had no idea exactly how tough. Or did she?

"Zantrax is a tough city," Paige pointed out. "You have to be tough to survive."

"I guess then that you do belong at the club because you've proved again and again that you're tough," Kate praised her, "with the things you've survived."

The loss of her baby and her ability to have any more children. And the loss of her husband. While she wasn't one of them—she did belong at Club Underground. She sighed.

"Well, you look exhausted," Kate said in her usual straightforward manner. "I'll let you get some rest."

But as Paige closed the door behind her friend, she caught a sound coming from Sebastian's windowless room. And she knew rest was the last thing she'd be getting.

Sebastian was at Ben's with his daughter—his *other* daughter. And from the look on Ben's face, Paige had assumed that the vampiress was dead. But maybe Marissa was like Sebastian—maybe she didn't stay dead.

Paige glanced around her living room, looking for something she could use as a weapon. But she had no wooden stakes on hand—nothing that could protect her from someone invincible.

"Who's there?" she called out.

Her pulse quickened with fear, but she forced herself to leave the sunshine of the living room for the dimly lit hall. No light at all emanated from Sebastian's windowless room; she'd intended to use it as a den before he'd moved in with her. She'd thought then that he'd had no place else to go, but now she realized he should have been anywhere else.

The thought of Sebastian leaving again—along with Addi and especially Ben—filled her with dread. She was a survivor, but a person could only be expected to survive so much.

"Who's there?" she called out again as she pushed open the door and stepped into the dark room.

"You don't need to know my name," a husky female voice replied from the thickest shadows. "You already know too much."

Paige shook her head. "I don't know what you're talking about."

"Sebastian Culver's daughter. Dr. Davison's ex-wife. There's no way that you haven't figured out the secret by now." The woman laughed as she moved closer to the light spilling in from the hall. Her dark hair and haunting eyes struck a chord in Paige's memory.

"I know you," she said. "You've been to the club."

"I've been Underground longer than you've been alive."

She needed to react, to pretend shock, since the woman appeared so young. But she'd always been better at hiding her feelings than feigning ones she didn't have.

"You're not going to bother lying to me?" the woman asked with a lilt of amusement and a flash of respect. "Your life depends on it, you know."

Panic clutched Paige's heart. "I know. But you would know, too, if I lied."

"I know more than most think," the vampiress cryptically claimed. "I know things that haven't even happened yet." Obviously she was psychic. "So I should have known..."

"That I would find out?"

"I knew that," she said. "That's why I tried to turn you once."

"It was *you*—in the office?" The person who had attacked Paige in the dark. She'd been so strong.

The woman nodded. "I respect the doctor. I didn't want him to lose you."

"*You* turned him," Paige realized with a flash of jealousy. Did the woman have more than respect for Ben? Did she love him?

"We need him," the vampiress explained.

"*I* need him." But she couldn't keep him.

"Then let me turn you."

"I asked him," Paige admitted. "But he doesn't want me to be part of this life of his." Anymore than he'd wanted her to be part of his other life.

"I have to turn you," the vampiress said, "or I have to kill you."

Chapter 19

In the exact spot in his garden where Ben had said goodbye to Paige several nights ago, he stood beside the pond, watching the water spew from the fountain and cascade over the rocks. He reached out and ran his fingertip, like Paige had, over their daughter's name engraved on the brass plate. His heart ached for his loss…Paige more than his baby.

He'd never really known Penny but for her kicks he'd felt through Paige's stomach. The vibration of her hiccups moving the stretched skin.

He missed what she could have been. He missed what Paige was: smart, beautiful, challenging... exciting. Stubborn.

"Hey?" Sebastian called out as he joined Ben in the backyard. "Are you out here?"

Ben considered remaining silent; he needed some time alone. But then Sebastian might need him more. "Back here."

The other man's shoes scuffed against the brick path leading to the pond. As he stepped to Ben's side, he uttered a reverent, "Oh..."

Ben cleared his throat. "Everything okay with Addi?"

A smile lifted Sebastian's lips. "She's doing better—great, actually."

"She's going to be fine," Ben assured him again.

"What about you?" his friend asked. "Are you going to be fine?"

"I don't know," he answered honestly. "I guess I'll get used to this life—eventually."

Sebastian snorted. "You've been living this life for years. You've been living Underground."

"Since I learned the secret."

"Long before that," his friend argued. "You've been living in the dark since you lost your mother. You're afraid to let anyone get too close to you. Afraid to let yourself be totally happy."

Ben snorted now. "Happiness never lasts. Why the hell would I set myself up for disappointment?"

"Damn you!" Sebastian bellowed. "When are you going to stop being a coward?"

Shock burst out of Ben in a short laugh. "What's gotten into you?"

"Too many years of minding my own damned business."

Ben laughed again. The last thing anyone would ever accuse Sebastian of doing was minding his own damned business. In addition to being a playboy, the bar manager was also the proverbial psychiatrist behind the bar—listening to and advising everyone on their problems. "Really?"

"Sure, I might offer my opinion…if someone asks for advice, but I haven't gotten into your business," Sebastian explained, "because I *respected* you too much."

From the way he'd twisted the word, that was obviously not a problem for him anymore. "And now you don't?"

"I don't respect anyone who keeps hurting the person who loves him most." He sighed. "Myself included."

"I never meant to hurt her," Ben insisted, his heart aching with all the pain he knew he'd caused her. "Hell, I shouldn't have fallen for her in the first place. I should have known that I would never be able to give her what she deserves."

"All she wants is your love," Sebastian said, "and you love her. I know you do. Hell, *she* knows you do."

"It's not enough," Ben insisted. "I can't offer her anything."

Sebastian shook his head. "Hell, you can offer her more now than you could before. You can give her eternity."

"No, I can't risk her life. If I try to turn her and fail…" He closed his eyes, but then images sprang to his mind, memories of all the mortals he'd been unable to save. He couldn't have Paige become one of those horrible memories.

"That's her decision to make."

Ben shook his head. "She doesn't know—what we do. She doesn't know what can go wrong. I can't let her take that risk for me."

"You're the one who needs to take the risk," Sebastian said. "You're the one who needs to finally figure out what the hell he wants. Paige already knows—she wants you."

"And I want Paige," he admitted. Even if he couldn't have her forever…he would take however long they could have together.

Sebastian gestured behind him, toward the pond and the fountain. "She's not here."

Ben closed his eyes and drew in a deep breath. "No, she's not." Only memories were here. "She's at the bar?"

"It's your turn to pick first round tonight," Lizzy told Paige.

"Paige?" Campbell called her name, bringing her out of her reverie. "Are you all right?"

"You're looking tired," Kate, blunt as ever, told her.

She hadn't been sleeping well the past several days, probably because she'd gotten used to not sleeping alone. Damn Ben. Damn his warm body wrapped around hers. Damn his strong arms holding her close. Damn him for denying her his love.

Renae, sitting in the corner, smiled a grim,

humorless smile. "I think it has something to do with Dr. Davison."

"Why would you think that?" Paige beat the detective to the question.

"When he bothers to show up at the hospital, he's even more pissed off than you," Renae shared. "He's scaring off all the staff and most of the patients. If they didn't have a bad heart before they came to see him, they do now."

"What happened between you two?" Lizzy asked.

"Nothing," Paige said. "We're divorced, remember? You drew up the papers."

"Just because you're divorced doesn't mean you don't still have feelings for each other," Lizzy said.

"Speaking from experience?" Paige asked.

Lizzy laughed. "Not mine."

"I haven't seen Ben myself," she said, bitterness slipping into her voice, turning it harsh to her own ears, "in quite a while."

"Then turn around," Kate suggested. "He's sitting at the bar."

If he wanted nothing to do with her, why had he come back here? Was Sebastian keeping him apprised of what was going on in *her* life?

* * *

As Paige walked down the hall toward her office, the skin between her shoulder blades tingled. Someone was watching her. Footsteps echoed hers. Someone was following her.

Her pulse quickened. Not with fear. She wasn't worried about Ingrid, or any other society member. She was worried, though—that she was about to get hurt again.

Her hand shaking, she struggled to unlock her office door. After she'd pushed it open, someone pushed her, his hand against her hip, over the threshold. Then he closed the door behind them. He had followed her from the bar.

"Ben—" She needed to tell him something… just in case Sebastian hadn't.

"Shut up," he told her, without anger, his lips lifted into a grin. "I'm done talking," he said as he reached for her.

Paige braced her hands against his chest, holding their bodies apart. "I don't understand…."

He had made it painfully clear that he didn't want her to be part of his new life.

"I'm done talking," he repeated. "I'm done thinking. I only want to feel." He leaned down, sliding his mouth across her cheek.

But she pulled back before he could kiss her. "Ben..."

"Shh..." he murmured as he cupped her face in his palms. "You're the only one who can make me feel, Paige."

Excitement rippled through her. She'd missed him. She'd missed him too much to question why he'd come after her even if it were for only this....

She slid her hands up, under his pale gray sweater, over the hair-dusted muscles of his chest. "You make me feel, too, Ben...."

Sometimes more than she wanted, more than she dared. Her zipper rasped as he pulled down the tab. Cool air touched the exposed skin on her back, until his hands slid over her, tugging her dress from her shoulders so that the silk gathered at her feet. Then he stepped back, studying her as she stood before him, clad only in thin lace panties.

"God, Paige, don't you ever wear a bra?"

"I can't in that dress," she explained as she stepped out of the pool of blue silk. She reached for him, tugging the sweater over his head before pulling at his belt.

His hands covered hers, shaking with his intensity, as he tore the belt through the loops of his black pants, letting them drop at his ankles, so he wore only black satin boxers. She'd bought him those a few Christmases ago.

The satin tented as he hardened. He pulled her back into his arms, then tugged her onto the couch with him. He tore her panties, pushed open the front of his boxers and drove into her heat. "Paige…"

"Yes, Ben," she said, panting as she took him deep. He leaned back against the couch, so she straddled his lap, riding him.

"Hmm?" he groaned, rolling his head against the burgundy leather. His hands closed around her hips, dragging her up and down his shaft, as he leaned forward again, his lips closing over one of her nipples, tugging gently with his teeth. A fang scraped across her skin.

She came, breaking apart in his arms. But he held her, driving her up and down until she came again. And again. Then, finally, he joined her, groaning her name as he spilled into her heat.

Then he sagged sideways, pulling her down with him onto the couch as he panted for breath.

Paige stretched as much as she could without falling off Ben and off the couch. "That was…"

"Too good to give up, Paige."

"We've been just about sex for the past four years, Ben. We both deserve more." They deserved *forever.*

He sighed his exasperation. "We've always been about more than sex, Paige."

"Guilt, pain, resentment," she said, "Yes, I guess we have been about more than sex."

"Paige, we've moved beyond that, beyond the past," he insisted. "But not beyond each other. We just proved that."

"We proved we're attracted to each other." She would probably always be attracted to him.

"We have more going on between us than attraction," Ben argued.

Love. At least on her part. She wasn't sure what he felt anymore. Hell, she'd never been sure of his feelings for her. "Ben…"

"We're friends, too."

She slid her naked breasts across his chest. "We're just friends?"

"What would Sebastian call it?" he asked. "Friends with benefits?"

She smiled. "I'm liking these benefits."

"Right now I'm trying to concentrate on the friend part, Paige," he said, his hands clenching her hips, holding her still. "I'm trying to remember what's best for you instead of acting just on what I want."

"What do you mean?"

"You asked me to turn you," he said, his voice raspy with emotion. "You said you wanted to be able to stay with me…"

"We're always going to be in each other's lives," she said. "It doesn't matter whether or not we're legally bound. We're emotionally bound." And nothing could break those bonds—now not even death.

"I love you, Paige," he said. "It's been killing me to stay away from you."

"Then you should have come for me." She gazed up at him, her eyes growing wet with unshed tears. "You shouldn't have waited." The days without him had seemed like months.

He groaned. "I didn't want to pressure you into making a decision *I* wanted for you—one that wasn't good for you."

"It's my decision to make," she pointed out. "I want to be with you. Always."

"You would take that risk," he asked, his voice deep with awe, "of turning—for me?"

"I love you, Ben," she said. "And there's no risk."

His hand trembled as he slid his fingertips across her cheek and down her throat. "It is dangerous. There were so many mortals that took that risk because they fell in love with a member of the society. But they didn't make it to eternity. They died."

"There's no risk anymore," Paige explained, "because I've already turned."

"What?" he asked, his dark eyes wide with shock. "How?" Then jealousy joined the shock. "Who?"

"Ingrid turned me," she said with a sigh, "like she turned you."

His hands tightened on her shoulders. "You could have died."

"She knows what she's doing." And somewhere deep inside the cynical vampiress beat the heart of a romantic. "She knows we belong together. Forever."

"Forever?" He shook his head. "I was such a fool for constantly pulling away from you. I was scared to care too much—scared that I'd have to leave again, like I went from foster home to foster home when I was a kid."

She'd known about his past; he'd shared the details with her but never before the emotions.

"Oh, Ben, I'm so sorry…." So sorry she hadn't understood how much her divorcing him must have hurt him and his fragile trust. "I'm so sorry…."

"I'm the one who's sorry. I regret every day we've spent apart, Paige," Ben said, his eyes dark with torment and remorse.

She stroked her fingers over his cheek. "Don't." Then she kissed his cheek. "Don't…" Her mouth slid across the stubble on his face until it covered his.

He kissed her back, his mouth hard and hungry against hers. His lips sucked, his tongue invaded, sliding in and out of her mouth. And their fangs clinked against each other's, like wine glasses in a toast.

"Paige…" he groaned.

She wanted more than his kiss. Even though they'd just made love, she hadn't known they'd actually been making love and not just having sex again. This time, for perhaps the first time, she knew exactly how he felt about her. He loved her. She slid her mouth from his, down his throat to his heart. She pressed her lips to where it pounded madly beneath his skin. With love for her.

His hands smoothed down her naked body, stroking over her breasts. He dipped his head and slid his mouth over one of the mounds. His tongue swiped across the nipple, again and again. Then he scraped the tip of a fang across the sensitive point.

She nipped at his shoulder, moaning his name against his skin. "Ben…"

His hands slid up the back of her naked thighs and over her butt. He cupped those mounds, as he had her breasts. Then he parted the folds of her femininity and dipped his fingers inside her.

She shuddered, her legs going weak. "Ben…"

His erection pressed against her hip, hard and ready for her. Silky skin over pulsing flesh. Paige closed her hands around him, stroking her fingers up and down his shaft. Then she pushed him back against the couch and lowered her head to his lap. She replaced her hand with her mouth, sliding her lips up and down. Her fangs scraped the side of his engorged cock.

His fingers clutched her hair, tangling in the strands as he held her to him. He groaned her name.

Licking him, she opened her eyes and peered up at him. "Come," she urged him.

But he pulled her away and dragged her up. Then he led her around to the arm of the couch, then pushed her, so that she bent over, her back to him. Paige braced her hands on the couch cushions, so that she didn't topple forward as he leaned over, filling his hands with her dangling breasts, nipping at her neck. His fangs slid over her skin, then penetrated as he also thrust deep inside her.

"Oh, God…" Tension spiraled inside her. Her legs trembled with the force of her desire for him. And she felt a pull from his fangs to her core as he sipped from her neck before pulling away.

"There you go, say my name," he teased, chuckling in her ear. His chest hair soft against her back, he held her tight as he pumped her. In and out. His thumbs flicked across her nipples, teasing them. His mouth nibbled her neck and bare shoulders. His breath blew hot and raspy against her ear. "Paige…"

He slid his hand down the front of her, over her stomach and lower. As he flicked his thumb across her clit, she came, her legs shaking. But he kept touching her, kept teasing her, until she came again. She clutched at the cushions, trying not to dissolve into a puddle beneath him.

He pounded into her relentlessly until he stiffened, then shouted his release. "Paige!"

He tipped them both onto the couch, so they sprawled, tangled in each other's arms, across the supple leather cushions.

She snuggled close, her face buried in his neck.

"Bite me," he invited her.

So she did, sinking her fangs into his skin. He groaned, and she pulled back. But he clutched his fingers in her hair the way he had earlier—urging her closer. So she bit him again and drank, sucking the sweet richness of his blood into her mouth. It trickled down her throat, filling her.

She pulled back, shuddering with another release. "Now I understand...."

His hand stroked over her back. "Yes, me, too…"

"And I understand you, too," she said, since he'd shared his emotions from his childhood with her. "But still I keep worrying that you're going to run off and leave me again."

"I may have kept leaving," he said, tightening his arms around her, pulling her closer to his side. "But I always came back. I could never stay away from you. I love you so much."

"I thought it was because I couldn't give you what you want," she admitted, "that I can't give you your own family, Ben."

"You already have," he said. "You've given me a loving wife. And a father-in-law who's become my best friend. And a beautiful little girl who will now always be part of our lives."

"More than part," Paige shared. "Sebastian wants us to be Addi's guardians now that her mother is dead."

Ben tensed. "Is he sure about this?"

"He had me draw up the legal adoption papers."

"But…" Ben's eyes widened with hope.

It was obvious that he already loved Addi; the child had slipped under his guard the same way Paige realized she had—despite his efforts to keep her out.

"How can he give her up?" he asked.

"The same way you tried giving me up," she said. "Because he loves her, he wants the best life for her. He thinks we can give that to her—that we can give her a stable, loving home. He'll stay part of her life." Just as he'd promised to stay a part of Paige's. "But he wants her to live with us."

"Are you sure about this?" Ben asked. "She's always going to be a child."

She nodded. "I love her…like I love you. Forever. No matter who or what we are, we'll always be together now." Paige finally believed that Ben was going nowhere—at least not without her and Addi. She had that family she'd always wanted and the man she had always loved and would love now for eternity.

* * * * *

Harlequin offers a romance for every mood!
See below for a sneak peek
from our paranormal romance line,
Silhouette® Nocturne™.
Enjoy a preview of REUNION
by USA TODAY *bestselling author*
Lindsay McKenna.

Aella closed her eyes and sensed a distinct shift, like movement from the world around her to the unseen world.

She opened her eyes. And had a slight shock at the man standing ten feet away. He wasn't just any man. Her heart leaped and pounded. He reminded her of a fierce warrior from an ancient civilization. Incan? She wasn't sure but she felt his deep power and masculinity.

I'm Aella. Are you the guardian of this sacred site? she asked, hoping her telepathy was strong.

Fox's entire body soared with joy. Fox struggled to put his personal pleasure aside.

Greetings, Aella. I'm the assistant guardian

to this sacred area. You may call me Fox. How can I be of service to you, Aella? he asked.

I'm searching for a green sphere. A legend says that the Emperor Pachacuti had seven emerald spheres created for the Emerald Key necklace. He had seven of his priestesses and priests travel the world to hide these spheres from evil forces. It is said that when all seven spheres are found, restrung and worn, that Light will return to the Earth. The fourth sphere is here, at your sacred site. Are you aware of it? Aella held her breath. She loved looking at him, especially his sensual mouth. The desire to kiss him came out of nowhere.

Fox was stunned by the request. *I know of the Emerald Key necklace because I served the emperor at the time it was created. However, I did not realize that one of the spheres is here.*

Aella felt sad. Why? Every time she looked at Fox, her heart felt as if it would tear out of her chest. *May I stay in touch with you as I work with this site?* she asked.

Of course. Fox wanted nothing more than to be here with her. To absorb her ephemeral beauty and hear her speak once more.

Aella's spirit lifted. What *was* this strange connection between them? Her curiosity was strong, but she had more pressing matters. In the next few days, Aella knew her life would change forever. How, she had no idea....

Look for REUNION
by USA TODAY *bestselling author*
Lindsay McKenna,
available April 2010,
only from Silhouette® Nocturne™.

HARLEQUIN®

INTRIGUE®

WILL THIS REUNITED FAMILY
BE STRONG ENOUGH TO EXPOSE
A LURKING KILLER?

FIND OUT IN THIS ALL-NEW
THRILLING TRILOGY FROM TOP
HARLEQUIN INTRIGUE AUTHOR

B.J. DANIELS

WHITEHORSE
MONTANA

Winchester Ranch

GUN-SHY BRIDE—*April 2010*

HITCHED—*May 2010*

TWELVE-GAUGE GUARDIAN—
June 2010

HARLEQUIN
Ambassadors

Want to share your passion for reading Harlequin® Books?

Become a Harlequin Ambassador!

Harlequin Ambassadors are a group of passionate and well-connected readers who are willing to share their joy of reading Harlequin® books with family and friends.

You'll be sent all the tools you need to spark great conversation, including free books!

All we ask is that you share the romance with your friends and family!

You'll also be invited to have a say in new book ideas and exchange opinions with women just like you!

To see if you qualify* to be a Harlequin Ambassador, please visit www.HarlequinAmbassadors.com.

*Please note that not everyone who applies to be a Harlequin Ambassador will qualify. For more information please visit www.HarlequinAmbassadors.com.

Thank you for your participation.

BAP09BPA

HARLEQUIN® Romance®

ROMANCE, RIVALRY
AND A FAMILY REUNITED

THE BRIDES
of
BELLA ROSA

William Valentine and his beloved wife, Lucia, live
a beautiful life together, but when his former love Rosa
and the secret family they had together resurface,
an instant rivalry is formed. Can these families
get through the past and come together as one?

Step into the world of Bella Rosa
beginning this April with

Beauty and the Reclusive Prince
by
RAYE MORGAN

Eight volumes to collect and treasure!

www.eHarlequin.com

HRI7650

OLIVIA GATES

BILLIONAIRE, M.D.

Dr. Rodrigo Valderrama has it all...
everything but the woman he's secretly
desired and despised. A woman forbidden
to him—his brother's widow.
And she's pregnant.

Cybele was injured in a plane crash
and lost her memory. All she knows is
she's falling for the doctor who has swept her
away to his estate to heal. If only the secrets
in his eyes didn't promise to tear
them forever apart.

Available March wherever you buy books.

Always Powerful, Passionate and Provocative.

SD73018

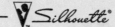
Silhouette®

SPECIAL EDITION

INTRODUCING A BRAND-NEW MINISERIES FROM *USA TODAY* BESTSELLING AUTHOR

KASEY MICHAELS

SECOND-CHANCE BRIDAL

At twenty-eight, widowed single mother Elizabeth Carstairs thinks she's left love behind forever....until she meets Will Hollingsbrook. Her sons' new baseball coach is the handsomest man she's ever seen—and the more time they spend together, the more undeniable the connection between them. But can Elizabeth leave the past behind and open her heart to a second chance at love?

FIND OUT IN

SUDDENLY A BRIDE

Available in April
wherever books are sold.

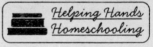

HER MEDITERRANEAN PLAYBOY

Sexy and dangerous—he wants you in his bed!

The sky is blue, the azure sea is crashing against the golden sand and the sun is hot.

The conditions are perfect for a scorching Mediterranean seduction from two irresistible untamed playboys!

Indulge your senses with these two delicious stories

A MISTRESS AT THE ITALIAN'S COMMAND
by *Melanie Milburne*

ITALIAN BOSS, HOUSEKEEPER MISTRESS
by *Kate Hewitt*

Available April 2010 from Harlequin Presents!

www.eHarlequin.com

REQUEST YOUR FREE BOOKS!
2 FREE NOVELS PLUS 2 FREE GIFTS!

Silhouette

n o c t u r n e

Dramatic and Sensual Tales of Paranormal Romance.